THE

NIGHTMARYS

THE NIGHTMARYS

Dan Poblocki

SCHOLASTIC INC.
New York Toronto London Auckland
Sydney Mexico City New Delhi Hong Kong

ISBN 978-0-545-38643-2

Published by Scholastic Inc., 557 Broadway, New York, NY 10012, by arrangement with Random House Children's Books, a division of Random House, Inc. SCHOLASTIC and associated logos are trademarks and/or registered trademarks of Scholastic Inc.

12 11 10 9 8 7 6 5 4 3 2 1 11 12 13 14 15 16/0

Printed in the U.S.A. 40

First Scholastic printing, September 2011

For Brendan and Emily

THE NIGHTMARYS

. . . the act of the passing generation
is the germ which may and must produce
good or evil fruit in a far-distant time . . .

—Nathaniel Hawthorne,
The House of the Seven Gables

Where does madness leave off and reality begin?
Is it possible that even my latest fear is sheer delusion?

—H. P. Lovecraft,
The Shadow over Innsmouth

"The girl's got sass," said the old man with a snarl.
"But that's never stopped me before."

—Ogden Kentwall,
The Clue of the Incomplete Corpse:
A Zelda Kite Mystery

INVISIBLE THINGS

PRELUDE

The Mayfair Apartments—
New Starkham, Massachusetts

On a Tuesday afternoon in early March, Zilpha Kindred prepared to do the laundry, as she'd done almost every Tuesday afternoon for the past forty years. This week, though, the old machine in her apartment was broken, so she left her schnauzer mix—an inquisitive little dog named Hepzibah—and wheeled the laundry basket to the elevator.

Downstairs, when the doors opened, the basement was almost entirely unfamiliar to the elderly woman, and a wave of unease overcame her. The corridor was longer than she recalled. The light was dim. The pipes hung from the low ceiling, craning at wicked angles every which way. A bitter scent lingered in the air. She was suddenly afraid and briefly considered returning to her apartment to call the local laundry service. But she had been doing her own laundry forever. And really, what did she have to be afraid of?

Zilpha walked for what seemed like an eternity before turning toward the laundry room. Its flickering fluorescent light instantly made her dizzy. She wished then that she had followed her earlier instinct and turned around. But she figured the job would be quick, and then she could go back upstairs and carry on with her day. In the meantime, she'd brought an old paperback to keep her company.

She filled and started the washer, then sat and waited and read her book. The water cycled. After a few minutes, Zilpha heard a thumping noise inside the machine. It became a hard, constant banging, as if she had accidentally dropped a shoe in with the detergent. When she opened the lid, she found the basin filled with soapy water. Whatever was making the sound was hidden at the bottom. With a huff, she rolled up her sleeve and reached in, digging through the wet clothes. Finding nothing unusual, she closed the lid. Whirring, the machine started up again.

But before she sat down, the thumping noise returned. She thought it might just be the shifting weight of the load working itself out somehow. She listened for a few more seconds before opening the lid again.

To her surprise, a red froth had boiled at the water's surface. Unlike the suds she'd seen earlier, there was a new substance, which reminded her of fat particles that rise to the top of a soup broth. Oily like meat. And worse, that bitter scent she encountered when the elevator door had opened was stronger now, as if coming from the red water. Her first instinct was that there was a problem with the machine or possibly the pipes. She decided to try another washer. Disgusted, she slowly reached into the basin to remove the pile of wet clothes.

But as Zilpha held the load, the laundry seemed to squirm like a fish. Alive. She shouted and dropped the pile back into the water, then stumbled away, her stomach in her throat.

Immediately, she tried to reason that she had imagined it. Briefly, she worried that Hepzibah had slipped inside the laundry bag upstairs, but then remembered kissing the dog goodbye at the apartment door. Zilpha could think of nothing, absolutely nothing, that might have provided a logical explanation for what she had just experienced, and so she reasoned that the sensation must have been in her head.

She eased her breathing, trying to calm her nerves. As she peered into the basin, where the clothes had sunk beneath the surface, her own dark reflection stared back from behind chunks of gristle. White globs of gore clung to her blank silhouette.

Then the lights flickered, and she could not bear another moment in that horrible basement. She decided to find Mario, the doorman, upstairs. She didn't care if she came across as a foolish old ninny. But when she headed back toward the long hallway, she heard something splash behind her. Zilpha turned and looked. The lights dimmed further, as if playing a game.

Then the entire washer lurched toward her so violently, the cords and pipes pulled out of the wall. The red water spilled over the edge of the basin and ran like blood down the front of the machine in a great gory wave.

That was enough to set her running. She did not look back until she reached the elevator and frantically pushed the button. The long hallway stared back at her quietly. Seconds later the door opened and she slipped into the car, pressing the button for the lobby.

But before the door slid shut, Zilpha saw a man come around the corner at the end of the hallway. She could not see his face, but she knew him nonetheless. He stood there in his tall dark overcoat watching her, as he had watched her in her memories for many years. As the door closed between them, she felt herself slipping away. By the time the elevator reached the lobby, she was unconscious.

She awoke in a hospital bed. Mario had found her and called an ambulance. The doctor explained that Zilpha's daughter and granddaughter were on their way from New Jersey to help take care of her, but this news did not calm the old woman. If what she'd seen in the basement was real, she

would have wished Sarah and Abigail to be as f
Starkham, Massachusetts, as possible. When she a
nurse for a phone so she might contact her daughter to
vince her to stay home, the nurse simply placed her hand ove
the old woman's own, trying to comfort her. Zilpha, however, knew that this was not the type of demon who was quelled with comfort.

Action must be taken, and soon.

This was not good. Not good at all.

1.

Timothy July first noticed the jars lining the top shelf along the side of room 117 at the beginning of the school year, but by mid-April he'd still not looked closer. The specimens inside the jars had been pickled decades earlier in an opaque and yellowish liquid by some forgotten alumnus of Paul Revere Middle School. Over the years, most of the labels had faded or peeled away from the glass, and so the true identity of the strange multilegged worms, the twisted slimy bodies of mammalian fetuses, and the hollow exoskeletons of beetles would be left to the imaginations of those students who bothered to crane their necks and peer into the dusty heights of the classroom's shadowy wall.

Until today, Timothy had taken no interest in them. No one had, not even Mr. Crane, Timothy's seventh-grade history teacher, over whose classroom the specimens watched silently and who was presently providing instruction for the next day's field trip.

"You'll work in pairs," said the teacher evenly, pacing in front of the long green chalkboard. "Together, you will choose a single artifact to study. I want ten pages from the two of you, illustrated in the manner of your choice—collage, drawings, charts, graphs, whatever—describing where your artifact is from, how it compares to the art of the era, and how . . ."

Timothy was not paying attention. Something in one of the jars was staring at him with a glassy black eye.

Stuart Chen leaned across the aisle and nudged him. Timothy jumped. "This is *so* lame," Stuart whispered. "I thought field trips were supposed to be fun. I can't believe he's actually going to make us do work."

Timothy glanced at his friend and distractedly grunted in agreement before turning back to the specimen in the jar. It's funny, he thought, how things that were once invisible suddenly become visible. The black-eyed creature continued to watch him, silent and unmoving, as if waiting for him to turn away so it could shift position . . . or maybe unscrew the lid. Timothy shuddered with the sudden thought that there might be countless other invisible things out there in the world that he'd never noticed before, watching him all the time.

"The *whole idea* is dumb," Stuart quietly droned on,

speaking over Mr. Crane's speech. "I mean, how are we supposed to know what to pick? Anything in the whole museum . . . ?" He glanced at Timothy. "You're going to have to choose for us. I don't really care."

Timothy nodded. "I don't care either," he whispered.

To his right, he heard a strange clicking sound. For a brief moment, he thought the thing in the jar had actually moved; then he quickly realized that the sound had not come from the shelves above but from two rows away in the back corner. The new girl was hiding something underneath her desk. She rested her left ankle on her right thigh and stared at something she held in the crook of her knee. Timothy heard the clicking sound again and watched as a small flame from a silver lighter burst at this new girl's fingertips.

"Let's get you paired up," said Mr. Crane, taking a notebook and pen from his desk.

As the teacher began to ask each student whom they would like to work with, Timothy watched the new girl in the last row continue to quietly flick the lighter open and closed. Like the specimen jars above her head, he'd never really paid attention to her before. She'd only been at the school for a month. She was quiet and didn't speak to anyone. She wore gray—sweatshirt, jeans, sneakers. If it weren't for her thick, messy red hair, she might have faded entirely into the wall. The next time she lit the lighter, to his surprise, she held it against her ankle. The flame raced up her white sock before extinguishing itself. Timothy couldn't have been more shocked if the thing in the jar had leapt off the top shelf behind her and landed in her lap.

"This is going to stink," Stuart said, not noticing the pyro in the corner. Timothy was too fascinated by what she was doing to pay any attention to his friend. Stuart poked Timothy in the shoulder and said, "Right?"

Suddenly, her brown eyes shifted toward him, and Timothy realized that he'd been caught.

"Abigail Tremens?"

The girl cupped the lighter in her fist and looked to the front of the classroom, where Mr. Crane was staring at her. "Yeah?" she said.

"Who would you like to work with?"

"Oh." Abigail let her eyes fall to the desk. "I . . . uh . . . don't know."

Mr. Crane peered across the blank faces of his students, who waited in silence for him to continue. "Would someone please volunteer to be Abigail's partner? We've all got to have a partner."

Abigail seemed to shrink into her seat with embarrassment.

The class did not answer.

Timothy absentmindedly scratched at his ear. Mr. Crane suddenly exclaimed, "Timothy July! Good."

Surprised, Timothy managed a weak whisper. "But—"

Mr. Crane didn't seem to notice. "Abigail and Timothy," he said pointedly, writing their names down in his notebook.

Timothy turned around. The girl stared at him, her mouth open in shock.

"Moving on. Stuart Chen, who would you like to work with?"

Timothy glanced apologetically at the boy who had been his usual partner, whenever they'd been given the opportunity, since kindergarten. But Stuart's mouth was pressed tightly shut; his face shone faintly red through his olive skin. He glared at Timothy, sending a different type of fire across the three-foot aisle.

2.

After sneaking away from the history classroom without speaking to Stuart, Timothy gathered books from his locker for his next class. His friend was angry, and Timothy knew he had every right to be. If their places were switched, he would have been just as upset.

After a moment, he decided it would be best to explain that it had been an accident. And if Stuart didn't get it—well, too bad.

Something was happening in Timothy's life that Stuart could not possibly understand, something his parents had made him promise to keep secret, a task he was finding more and more difficult with every passing day.

He'd just taken his hand out of the locker when the door slammed shut. Timothy leapt backward to find Stuart standing beside the locker, smiling strangely. After a few silent seconds, Timothy managed to say, "Hey, I'm really sorry about the whole partner thing. It was—"

"A little late for that now," Stuart interrupted. "You could have said something to Mr. Crane during class."

"I—I said I was sorry," said Timothy. "We'll be partners next time. Promise."

"Fat Carla," said Stuart, his eyes darkening. "How would *you* like to be working with Fat Carla?"

"I'd like it all right." This was what he'd been afraid of.

"Liar."

Timothy felt his face start to burn. "You're kinda being unfair, don't you think? It wasn't my fault. Plus, during class, you kept saying how lame the project was going to be."

"That's 'cause it *is* going to be lame," said Stuart. "But at least we would have been in it together."

Something was bubbling deep inside Timothy. Something he'd wanted to say to Stuart for a while now. "Maybe it'll be good to try something different."

"Different? What do you mean—*different*?"

"Stuart," Timothy whispered. "Sometimes you can be . . ."

"Be what?" Stuart's smile finally dropped away.

"Not everything is lame. Not everyone is ugly and stupid. In fact, I think the field trip tomorrow might be fun. You're always so . . . I just think . . . maybe it would be a good idea . . ."

"What would be a good idea?" Stuart's voice hardened.

"To work with a different partner on this project," said Timothy, clutching his math book. "That's all I'm saying."

"Oh, *that's* all you're saying?"

"I gotta get to class." Timothy started to back away, heading toward the math wing.

"You wanna talk about *different*?" said Stuart, following him. "You should know. You've been acting different ever since . . . I don't know when."

Timothy felt his face flush deeper. He knew why he'd been acting differently lately, but he hadn't figured out a way to tell Stuart without breaking his promise to his parents. "Look, just forget it," Timothy said. "I'll see you later."

"Whatever," said Stuart, before turning around and walking away.

Timothy closed his eyes for a moment, trying to shake away the horrible sensation in his head. But he didn't have the energy to think about Stuart and all his stupid crap.

He was about to head into his math class when someone grabbed his arm, jerking him to a stop. Abigail Tremens stood behind him, glaring with her deep brown eyes. She quickly crossed her arms over her chest.

"So . . . you think you're, like . . . my boyfriend now?" she mumbled.

Timothy felt like she'd slapped his face. "Uh . . . no."

"Good. 'Cause I don't need a boy to rescue me or anything.

I don't need a boyfriend. I don't need a friend. I don't need anything. Okay? I'm fine by myself."

"Mr. Crane said we all needed a partner. Now you have one. What's the big deal?"

Abigail stared at him for another moment before saying, "Just stay away from me."

3.

At the end of the day, despite the drizzle spitting against the school's front doors, Timothy purposely missed the bus home. He simply waited in the boys' bathroom until a little after three o'clock, when he knew the long line of buses would clear away from the main entrance of the school. He couldn't imagine sitting next to Stuart for the entire ride back to Edgehill Road.

For a while now, their friendship had felt weird; the shape of their history was a puzzle piece that no longer fit the empty space Timothy knew was inside him. It was odd—they both still liked to play video games. They watched the same television shows. Their comic books had become so mixed-up over the past few years, it was no longer possible to distinguish which belonged to whom. Together, the boys attended swim-team practice three nights a week and every other Saturday morning. And their parents had always been close, at least until recently.

Everything had changed when Timothy's brother Ben's unit had been sent away. The Chens didn't understand how the Julys could let Ben enlist during such dangerous times. The Julys didn't think it was their neighbors' business.

When Timothy asked his brother about his decision, Ben explained that, though he was terrified to go, it was his way of finding a sense of order in all the world's chaos. This was something Ben could *do*: find a little light in the darkness. Make a decision. Accomplish something. It was Ben's way of dealing with his fear, with the uncertainty of war and politics and all those other big ideas that Timothy hadn't yet begun to think about.

After Ben went overseas, those words had become like a mantra to Timothy. *Find order in chaos. The little light in the darkness.* The words were a comfort. They gave him hope.

Timothy opened the bathroom door and peered into the hallway. A few footsteps echoed through the now-quiet corridors of the school, but he couldn't see anyone. With nothing and no one to stop him, Timothy zipped up his jacket and hiked his book bag high onto his shoulders before making his way toward the school's front entrance and out into the wet afternoon.

* * *

Paul Revere Middle School was a redbrick Victorian monstrosity of a building that sat on the edge of downtown New Starkham, well away from the river and the bridge, past College Ridge, bordered on the east by numerous factories and warehouses.

As Timothy pushed his way into the blustering wind up Johnson Street, he could see the silhouettes of the seven gothic spires, which marked New Starkham College, peeking over the hill's horizon. New Starkham students passed Timothy on the sidewalk in small clusters, bundled against the unseasonable chill. They laughed at nothing in particular as they made their way up the street.

In a couple of weeks, their final exams would be done. For the college students, graduation happened at the beginning of May. Lucky, thought Timothy. Classes at Paul Revere didn't let out until the end of June. As he turned right onto Edgehill Road, Timothy shuddered at the realization that only a year ago, Ben had made his own trip across the stage in the high school auditorium to receive his diploma. So much had changed since then.

Timothy trudged several blocks along the tree-lined street, continuing up the hill, passing the quiet houses on either side, until he reached the wooded area on the left that dropped away from the road. A battered silver guardrail hugged the sharp curve—the "edge" part of Edgehill Road.

From there, a long, covered staircase descended the steep wooded hill to the college's athletic fields at the bottom.

At the end of the guardrail, Timothy came upon the entrance to the stairs. The bluffs across the river looked as sullen and cold as Timothy felt, the clouds above darkening in papier-mâché strips. The only color Timothy could see came from inside the stairs' graffiti-covered walls.

The staircase had been nicknamed the Dragon Stairs by students and faculty who lived off campus in Timothy's neighborhood. Several years ago, someone had painted an immense Chinese dragon onto one wall, stretching from the bottom stair to the top, where its swirling eyes rolled back into its head as if in the throes of a terrible dream. Timothy thought the dragon was cool, but its eyes were creepy. He felt like he might fall into them and keep falling forever. It was an irrational fear, like in nightmares, the way everyday objects can instantly become ominous. Stuart teased him about it, pretending to chortle in the dragon's high-pitched voice, telling Timothy, "I'm going to eat you up." Then they'd laugh together, turn up Beech Nut Street, and race home.

Now, at the top of the stairs, the monster's black-and-white pinwheel pupils reminded Timothy of the thing that had been watching him from inside the jar back in Mr. Crane's classroom. He suddenly found himself thinking about the new girl, Abigail Tremens, who would be his project partner during the field trip to the museum tomorrow. In his head,

Timothy could see Abigail's eyes boring into his own, only now, instead of brown, they had turned the black and white of the Chinese dragon. *Stay away from me,* they growled.

Timothy shook his head and turned away.

Why had she been so angry? he wondered.

Maybe invisible things don't like being seen.

Timothy was nearly soaked by the time he reached the front porch of his small gray house. He thought of the last time he walked home alone from school. Last week, when Stuart was at a doctor's appointment, Timothy had found a big black car parked in his driveway. Inside, the men in uniforms had already told his mother about Ben's injuries.

Today there was no car. Timothy brushed a drip of water from his forehead. A cough came from the house next door. He didn't even need to look to know that Stuart was watching him. He took a deep breath and turned around, ready to confront his best friend, once more hoping they could just laugh it off the way they usually did.

But Stuart had already gone. The slam of the screen door rang out across their shared yard. The Chens' front porch was empty. Unless Stuart had figured out a way to become invisible himself, he wasn't there, wasn't watching.

4.

Inside, Timothy ripped off his wet jacket and threw it over the banister at the bottom of the stairs. Then he dropped his bag onto the wooden bench in the hallway. Timothy noticed his mother standing in the kitchen down the hall, leaning her head against the cabinet next to the sink. "Hi, Mom," he called. "Guess what?" He waited for her to turn around, but she didn't, so he continued, "I saw a girl light her foot on fire today."

"That's nice, honey" was his mother's muffled reply. A few seconds later, when she did turn around, her face was drawn. "I'm going to make dinner," she said. "Your father should be home soon." She looked older than usual and terribly sad.

"Mom?" Timothy tried again. She turned on the sink. "When can we talk to people about what happened to Ben?"

"Soon, honey." She turned away from him. "When we know a little more about . . ." She washed her hands.

"About what?" he asked cautiously. He waited and waited, but the only answer that came from the kitchen was the sound of clinking dishes.

Later that night, when Timothy was in bed, through the wall, he could hear his parents arguing. Outside, the wind had blown away the clouds, so the moon shone brightly onto his quilt. The house rocked against a particularly powerful gust.

His parents were talking about Ben. Timothy was upset that they had each other to confide in but he had no one. And when he tried to talk to them about it, they pretended he wasn't there.

It was after midnight, and he was awake, huddled under his blanket, thinking about the afternoon's events, trying to block out his parents' voices. If he didn't get to sleep soon, he might sleep through his alarm in the morning. Despite Stuart and Abigail, he was actually looking forward to the field trip.

In his parents' room, the closet door slammed, and Timothy heard his mother say, "Quiet, you'll wake him up."

He noticed that his own closet light was on. At the base of the door, a small white line reflected onto the dark wood floor. The light had not been on when he'd gotten into bed an hour earlier.

Someone flushed the toilet down the hall. "Mom?" Timothy called. No answer. "Dad?"

Ordinarily, Timothy wouldn't have thought twice about getting up and turning off the light, but recently he'd begun to notice things he'd never noticed before. Invisible things. And what if one of those invisible things was behind the door?

"Mom?" Timothy tried again. But the rest of the house was now dead, and he was left alone with the moonlight, and the wind outside the window, and the weight of his quilt. And the light behind his closet door.

Barefoot, shivering, Timothy stepped out of bed. No one and nothing would be in there, he told himself. Scary things never happened when you were expecting them to; scary things always came out of nowhere to surprise you. He grasped the doorknob and slowly turned it. When it wouldn't turn any more, Timothy heaved a sigh and swung the door open. What he saw made him nearly wet his pants.

Inside the closet was a large glass jar like the ones from his history classroom. The jar was taller than Timothy, covered with dust and filled with a cloudy yellow liquid. A large black lid was hanging loosely over the rim. Something dark floated near the bottom of the jar. The object began to move.

Through the smudged glass, drifting in the liquid, two arms and a leg came into view. They looked human. After a few seconds, the thing inside the jar finally came close enough for Timothy to distinguish the military emblem on its decaying sleeve. Suddenly, as if blessed with life, the dark shape raised its hands, pressed them to the jar, and brought its face against the glass.

It wasn't an It.

It was a He.

Timothy's brother, Ben, opened his mouth wide and showed him his purple swollen tongue.

Timothy screamed.

Ben stared at him with big eyes the same color as the Chinese dragon, the same color as the specimen in Timothy's classroom. Swirling. Black. Mad.

Ben reached up and knocked the lid to the ground. It clattered against the hardwood floor and spiraled past Timothy in a long, continuous cymbal crash. With pale wrinkled hands, Ben grasped the rim of the jar and pulled himself up from the liquid. He raised his head above the rim, took a deep howling gasp, and smiled wide, showing a mouthful of dead brown teeth.

Timothy jerked awake. He sat up. His room was dark. The closet door was closed and the light was off. It had never been on. His bedroom walls solidified and the furnace hummed somewhere below the floor. Timothy could hear his father snoring in the next room.

Sheesh.

He'd been having nightmares ever since Ben went away.

This was by far the scariest. But it was just a nightmare. Not real. And that was a comfort.

After a while, the moon moved back behind the clouds, and the nightmare began to fade away. By the time Timothy's head hit the pillow again, he'd nearly forgotten all about it. Nearly.

EDGE OF DOOM

INTERLUDE

New Starkham Hospital—
New Starkham, Massachusetts

Byron Flanders had suffered several heart attacks since retiring from his career as the New Starkham district attorney twenty years ago, but this most recent one had been the worst. The night before his bypass surgery, he was having trouble sleeping. He lay in his private hospital bed hooked up to all sorts of tubes and wires, the weak fluorescent light on the wall barely illuminating the small mattress. He was cold. The pulsing of the heart monitor was like water torture. *Beep. Beep. Beep.*

He'd paged the nurse for the third time in several minutes to try and get an extra blanket, but no one had responded. He'd already struggled to close the curtain that surrounded his bed to stop the air conditioner from blowing at him, but it was not helping. Byron Flanders was not used to waiting, and he was becoming annoyed.

Throughout his life, Byron got what he wanted. In the courtroom, he'd earned himself the nickname "the Hammerhead," as in shark. If you were accused of a crime, and the Hammerhead decided you were guilty, he usually found a way to put you away. His tactics were usually legal, but not always. He figured, when you have a job to do, you do it. You get it done. No matter what.

Now, if only the nurses had the same philosophy . . .

As he reached out for the call button again, a draft blew against the curtain, as if someone had opened the door to his room. Finally . . .

"Nurse!" Byron called. "I need a blanket. It's freezing in here!" The curtain went still, but no one answered. "Nurse?" he tried again. "Hello?" Goose bumps broke out all over his frail body, and this time, it had nothing to do with the air conditioner. He could feel a presence. Someone was in the room with him.

He'd said goodbye to his children earlier that evening, but maybe one of them had come back.

The curtain at the foot of his bed was moving, as if someone were scratching at it from the other side. "Is anyone there?" he asked, though he wasn't certain he wanted an answer. Suddenly, the scratching moved. Now it was directly to his right, next to the bed stand. Then the scratching moved again, to the opposite side of the bed. Suddenly, the entire curtain began to ripple, as if hundreds of fingers were dragging against the cloth. Eventually, the fingers clenched, balling up the fabric. They began to pull downward, putting pressure on the silver bearings that attached the curtain to the long slider on the ceiling.

The heart monitor began to beep faster and faster. Though it pained him, the old man cried out as loud as he could, "Nurse!"

The curtain was torn down, fluttering like a magician's cape to the floor. Now Byron could see that the room was filled with people. He shrieked. Their faces were illuminated by that faint fluorescent light, making them all appear sicker than himself. He knew them. They were the criminals he'd helped convict over the course of his life. None of them spoke. None of them moved. They stood around his bed and watched as he wet himself. Then, from the middle of the group, Byron saw a man in a long gray overcoat step forward. He smiled.

"Christian? Is that you?" Byron whimpered. "You . . . you're dead," he added, pathetically. "You're *all* dead."

A new pain bloomed in his chest, like a bright red rosebush full of pricker thorns. The man in the overcoat smiled wider and chuckled as Byron's vision blurred. He tried one last time to call for the nurse as his life slipped away into darkness, and the heart monitor finally stopped its awful *beep-beep-beeping*, instead filling the room with a plain and soothing hum.

5.

On the morning of the field trip, Mr. Crane lined up his students in the hallway. Several yellow buses waited in the fog in front of the school. The classes piled in. To Timothy's surprise, Stuart smiled as he made his way up the aisle and slipped into the seat beside him. Tufts of dark hair stuck up from Stuart's head, his eyes were still puffy from sleep, and some sort of pale milky crust had been left from breakfast just below his lower lip. As usual. But after yesterday's fight, Timothy didn't expect everything to be fine between them.

"Oh my God," said Stuart, "you wouldn't believe what happened last night." He didn't wait for a response. "You know the part in *Wraith Wars* where Fristor has to climb the cliff with his bare hands and we can never get to the top without losing almost all of our life force because the giant

Nemcaws keep flying at our heads and trying to peck out our eyes?"

"Sure," Timothy answered tentatively. "That part's wicked hard." He didn't trust that Stuart wasn't still mad at him.

"Not anymore," Stuart continued. "When I was about halfway up the rock, before the Nemcaws got there, I noticed that there was this ledge sticking out of the cliff way off to

the right of the screen. So I swung myself over to it, and guess what I found?"

Timothy shook his head and shrugged.

"A cave!" Stuart said, throwing his hands into the air. "It was *so* amazing. The walls were carved with all these weird symbols and it was really dark and I could barely see."

Stuart paused in his story for a moment, and Timothy noticed the red-haired girl come onto the bus. She didn't look at anyone. Stuart didn't say anything about her, but Timothy watched as something clicked inside his friend, as if Stuart had checked an item off a mental list. Stuart simply blinked, then began again. "So I was crawling into the darkness and all of a sudden, I saw this huge claw coming toward me."

Abigail made her way to the back of the bus and slid into the last empty seat near them.

"I ducked out of the way, then smashed it with my sword."

"That's awesome," said Timothy, trying to sound excited.

The bus shuddered as the driver started the engine. Mr. Crane strolled down the aisle taking a final head count, before the bus finally lurched forward into the mist.

The ride up the hill toward the river was bumpy. Abigail Tremens hung her head. Timothy could hear the same faint clicking sound he'd heard yesterday in class, the harsh grind of the silver lighter's wheel striking the flint. He wondered if she had on her fireproof socks again.

The bus crossed onto the Taft Bridge. Once over the river, they passed the Little Husketomic Lighthouse, perched on an outcropping of steep rock upstream from the bridge. A white light flashed dully through the mist and a horn sounded, warning boats to keep their distance. Moments later, the bus veered off the highway and exited onto a small road. They drove for several minutes through a pale forest of birch trees. Everyone stared straight ahead as the Husketomic Museum appeared in the distance, looking like a temple out of ancient Greece.

"This is going to be—" Stuart started to say, but when Timothy glared at him, apparently he decided not to finish his sentence.

Once outside, in the parking lot, Mr. Crane asked everyone to partner up. To Timothy's surprise, he noticed a redheaded presence standing next to him. After what Abigail had said yesterday afternoon, he'd expected her to simply ignore him all day. Or punch him.

Mr. Crane led the group up the museum's front steps, through the teethlike columns, and into the mouth of the building. Before Timothy passed through the doors, he heard the faraway foghorn cry out once more, greeting the morning with another warning.

6.

Inside, their tour leader, a gap-toothed young woman in a tweed jacket, brought the group to a small room where they hung their damp coats. "Keep those eyes open for your project," said Mr. Crane.

The museum was endless. Several rooms were packed entirely with headless and armless white marble torsos. In other rooms, giant canvases stretched from floor to ceiling and were so old, tiny cracks formed in the paint. There were rooms filled with tall glaring totem poles and long wooden canoes; rooms with mysterious obelisks carved with hieroglyphs; hallways of glass cases stuffed with tiny pieces of colorful ancient jewelry.

As Timothy followed the tour, though, he found himself staring more at Abigail than at the artwork on the walls or in the cases. She was strange and quiet, walking as if in a dream or a daze, as if she was seeing the world in a way the rest of them couldn't.

Eventually, in one small dark room, he came upon a large poster on the wall that read, *Magic and Religion in Prehistoric Scandinavia.* Magic? Maybe, Timothy figured, they could choose one of these artifacts for their project. Glancing into a glass case nearby, he read a small placard that was supposed to

mark an ancient "magical" jawbone with a "primitive artificial tooth." The placard explained that the jawbone was connected with a dark goddess called the Daughter of Chaos. The bone was actually used as a tool during revenge rituals. The description continued, "The myths explain that a member of the tribe would hold the jawbone in his fist, name the person he wanted revenge upon, and a curse would be placed. The tribe believed that this curse made the victim see all his worst fears come true. Whoever held the bone could read the victim's mind and use the victim's fear to force him to betray an ally, attack a family member, or even destroy himself."

This artifact sounded totally amazing.

"Too bad," said a voice next to Timothy. To his surprise, he found that Abigail had been standing beside him, reading along.

"Too bad what?" said Timothy.

She nodded at the case, where the jawbone was supposed to be. In its place was a piece of paper that read:

"Would have been a good one. Don't you think?"

The woman in the tweed jacket led the class to one particularly cavernous room on the fourth floor. While the group listened to the tour guide's speech on the far side of the room, Timothy and Abigail stopped in the opposite corner and stared at a large dark canvas.

"Many of the most recent acquisitions were brought to the museum by our new director," said the woman. "We're quite lucky to have such a distinguished—"

Someone in the group made a farting sound, and the class burst into laughter.

But Timothy barely registered the noise. His mind was elsewhere.

The painting on the wall in the far corner was an enormous landscape. In the sky, at the canvas edges, clouds roiled, blacker than night. Below the clouds, a stone temple, which resembled the museum's own classical façade, trembled on the precipice of a deep chasm from which spewed brilliant red flames. On the cliff's edge, a man stood, dressed in black robes, arms raised, face turned in anguish toward the sky. In the center of the painting, just above the burning pit, the clouds glowed yellow, as if answering him. The title of the painting, noted on a small placard to the right of the canvas, was *The Edge of Doom.*

Abigail pointed at the painting, then, almost smiling, she said, "That's the one. It's so amazing." She turned to look at him.

"Yeah," said Timothy. "Really cool." He pointed at the man in the center of the painting. "What do you think that guy's saying?" He made his voice really low and grunted, "Um, I could use a little help here? Hello? Anyone?"

Mr. Crane interrupted from across the room. "You may break into your pairs for one last wander around the museum. Meet in the coatroom in an hour, and don't be late. The bus leaves promptly at noon."

Timothy turned back to find Abigail now glaring at him.

"What?" he asked. "What did I say?"

"Are you making fun of me?" Abigail said.

"About what?"

"Because I actually *like* the painting." Her eyes were filled with fire. For some reason, Timothy remembered her socks. Even though it was a stupid thought, he couldn't help but laugh a little bit. This only made the fire in her eyes grow brighter. "You're laughing at me?"

"No, I'm not laughing at you," Timothy tried to explain, pointing at the painting. "I'm laughing because . . ." *You keep trying to light yourself on fire,* his brain finished the sentence silently. But he couldn't say that to her, at least not now, while she looked like she wanted to kill him.

"You know what?" said Abigail. "Just forget it. Do the project by your stupid self. I don't care." She turned around to face *The Edge of Doom.*

After a few seconds, Timothy tried again. "I *said* it was really cool. How is that making fun of you?"

Abigail continued to stare at the painting, her arms hugging her torso. Timothy took a deep breath. This wasn't what he'd expected to happen.

"I'm sorry you thought I was making fun of you."

Without turning around, Abigail said, "You're sorry for making fun of me or you're sorry I *thought* you were making fun of me?"

"I wasn't making fun of you," Timothy answered as simply as he could. "I was just being a . . . butt-munch."

Finally, Abigail turned around, amused. After a few moments, she said, "A butt-munch? No. I'd say more of a . . . fart-slap."

Timothy laughed. *Fart-slap* was funnier than anything Stuart had ever come up with. Abigail chuckled too, then stepped closer to the painting. "What do we have to do? Make a chart or a graph or something?"

"I have no clue."

"I actually wasn't paying attention in class at all."

"I noticed," said Timothy. He could almost hear the click of her little lighter in his memory. "I mean, none of us were."

"Hey, Abigail!" a voice called into the room, resonating off the walls.

What happened next, happened so quickly, it took Timothy several seconds to even realize he was soaking wet. Abigail screamed. Timothy jumped and nearly slipped as his feet slid across the now-slick marble floor. When he spun around, he saw Abigail holding out her arms helplessly in front of herself. Her T-shirt was drenched. Her face was dripping with water, and her long red hair was plastered to her head.

"What the heck just happened?" Timothy heard himself say.

Some of the class had gathered and were staring and pointing. Laughter echoed throughout the cavernous room. Other museum guests had stopped to watch the commotion too. Timothy felt his face turning red as he noticed a small blue dot on the floor next to his foot. It looked like a thin piece of peeled paint, or maybe rubber. He kicked at it, almost unconsciously, and the answer came to him.

A water balloon.

Someone had thrown a water balloon at Abigail.

Stuart.

Timothy wanted to scream. Carla, Stuart's partner, stood next to Mandy and Karen in the doorway, but the culprit was gone.

"Are you okay?" he said to Abigail instead. She only stood there, dangling her arms, looking like a wet cat. She shook her head slightly, but Timothy couldn't tell if she was just trying to dry off.

Through the crowd of his classmates, Timothy watched a couple of security guards push their way toward him. He glanced at *The Edge of Doom*. Droplets of water clung to the black clouds and the open chasm, as if the painting itself had started to precipitate.

Oops.

Before the two large men in uniform could make their way to him, Timothy felt Abigail rush past him, through the door on the far side of the room. "Wait," Timothy called, running after her, trying not to slip on the wet floor. Peeking over his shoulder, he noticed that one security guard had stopped to examine the wet painting. The other guard, however, was coming after them.

7.

Through the doorway, Timothy went to the large staircase spiraling into the lower levels of the museum. Pausing briefly to peer over the brass railing, he noticed a quickly moving shadow descending, fluttering against the white marble steps, already one flight down. "Abigail!" he called. Footsteps were coming up close behind him. Timothy hurried toward the top step.

He ran so fast that the stairs seemed to disappear beneath his feet. He descended into the bowels of the building, aware that he'd finally breached the ground level and was now chasing Abigail into the basement. When he ran out of stairs, a darkened hallway stretched before him. The shadows at the far end of the hallway seemed to shiver, or maybe that was just Timothy, cold and winded and wet.

Timothy listened. He could still hear footsteps, but he wasn't entirely certain whether they were in front of him or above him. He kept going. Halfway down the hall, Timothy noticed movement in a lighted doorway. This room was long and thin with a low ceiling. On the opposite wall was another doorway. A red velvet rope hung across it. A small sign, perched in the center on a silver pole, read: ADMINISTRATIVE OFFICES—CLOSED TO THE PUBLIC.

Timothy entered the room. He wandered past small luminescent gold objects, Aztec creations, which were crowded onto the shelves of several display cases. A few small idols with wide, toothy smiles looked ready to laugh . . . or bite.

Halfway through the room, Timothy heard a sniff. Looking down, he could see Abigail's foot sticking out from behind one of the cases. "Abigail, are you okay?" he asked.

Her foot disappeared behind the case. She peered at him. Her face was blotchy with tears. Her shirt was still soaking wet, and her hair was a tangled mess. "Hell," she said. "Just . . . go away."

Timothy bent down anyway. "Stuart got me pretty good too," he said. He pointed at his darkened shirt.

"Wow," said Abigail. She looked at Timothy and seemed to really see him. Her face changed, and in her fiery eyes, he noticed recognition, as if she had suddenly stumbled upon a mirror. "You're totally drenched."

"Freakin' Stuart Chen." Timothy chuckled. "*He's* the freakin' fart-slap. Better watch himself at swim practice tonight. His towel might just end up in the pool."

They stared at each other for several seconds, surrounded by the grinning golden idols, before Timothy felt laughter creeping up from the bottom of his stomach. Before he knew it, they were both giggling. It felt good to laugh. The laughter grew the more he tried to contain it. He tried to be quiet. But soon, it was impossible to stop. Abigail appeared to have the same problem. Her shoulders hitched and quaked, but a few seconds later, as their laughter began to die down, she covered her face in her hands. Now she was crying.

Timothy didn't know what to do. When he'd come after her, he hadn't thought about what might happen next. He reached out and touched her shoulder. "Abigail, don't worry about it," he said. "It's not worth it. People are just . . . stupid and mean."

Through her hands, she said, "It's your fault."

It took a few seconds for him to register her statement. "My fault?"

Her voice was muffled through her fingers, but he could hear her say, "If you hadn't picked me for a partner, this wouldn't have happened. No one would have noticed me, and everything would have been fine."

"What do you mean, no one would have noticed you?"

Finally, she took her hands away from her face. Her eyes were red rimmed and swollen. "You don't understand."

"Well then, tell me."

"When no one notices you, stuff like this doesn't happen."

Out of the corner of his eye, Timothy could see something moving. It stood beyond the dark door on his left, behind the red velvet rope in front of the administrative offices. When Timothy looked at it straight on, it quickly moved backward into the soupy black shadows. Whatever was there had been watching them for some time. Timothy thought he could hear it whispering something to itself.

"Just . . . go back to the rest of the class," said Abigail. If she noticed the shape in the hallway, she didn't want Timothy to know. "I'll come find you later. I want to be by myself right now." She turned away from him, hiding her face again.

Before he could respond, the room seemed to grow darker. At the same time, the light reflecting off the gold pieces in the cases appeared to grow brighter. Timothy stared into the face of a small, ghastly gold skull sitting on the shelf to the left of Abigail's shoulder.

"I'll be fine," he heard Abigail say, as if from far away.

He could not answer her. The rest of the room faded. Soon, only the glowing gold pieces were left. The skull stared at him, its eyes widening like dark whirlpools. When he looked away, to his horror, every other artifact on the shelves was facing him too. The mouths of the idols slowly opened and closed, as if chanting silent prayers.

Timothy covered his mouth and closed his eyes.

Last night's dream rushed back at him—Ben gasping for breath inside the jar. Timothy let out a whimper and opened his eyes again. The idols continued to stare at him. He was tempted to run, but he couldn't leave Abigail here alone. Instinctively, he grasped her shoulder and spun her around to demand that they go, when he realized that half-hidden underneath Abigail's tangled mess of red hair was a horrible skull-like grimace, grinning like the golden idols in the glass cases.

The Abigail-thing simply reached up, touched his cheek with bony fingertips, and forced him to look into the darkness near the administrative offices hallway. "Get out of here," she whispered. But Timothy couldn't move.

Lit dimly by the golden idols' unnatural glow was a tall man. He appeared to be cloaked in a long coat, a brimmed hat perched on his head, shiny black wingtip shoes on his feet. Timothy could not make out any other features, but the sight of these simple few shrank his skin to his bones. The man appeared to be staring at him. However, as Timothy stared back, unable now to turn away or even contemplate what might be happening, he slowly understood that the shadow man was not in fact staring at him, but at something beyond him, behind him, in the doorway on the opposite side of this strange room.

"Abigail?"

The voice seemed to throw the horror world of this room into tumult, and before Timothy could even blink, the shadows had disappeared, the gold idols had become lifeless, and Abigail had become herself again.

She turned toward the voice, which had come from the entry opposite the velvet rope, and this time it was her turn to wear an expression of shock. There stood an old woman.

Her voice wavering, Abigail replied, "Gramma? What are you doing here?"

8.

The old woman was tall. She wore a knee-length navy peacoat, a floral blouse, and polyester pants. Tufts of dark gray hair curled out from underneath a floppy houndstooth hat, the brim of which fell in waves around the edge of her face like the petals of a flower. She had a long, regal nose and large, wide-set brown eyes. She seemed truly surprised, almost shocked, to find Timothy and Abigail in the basement of the museum.

"What am *I* doing here?" said the woman addressed as "Gramma." "My dear, I feel I should ask you the same thing. Aren't you supposed to be in school?" She sounded more confused than concerned, as if she were worried that she might be seeing things. Timothy knew the feeling.

The sight of the woman in the entrance had been enough

to make Timothy momentarily forget about the shadowy figure in the other door. But when he heard brisk footsteps scuffing away, he turned his head once more to look. The tall man in the long overcoat was gone, but a small book lay on the floor where he had stood.

Had he imagined the whole thing? Was he imagining still?

"My class is here on a field trip today," said Abigail. "Mom signed the permission slip last week. Remember?" She ran to meet the woman in the doorway, leaving Timothy alone among the glass cases and wide-eyed artifacts.

He could not take his eyes off the book on the floor beyond the rope. He cautiously moved toward it. It lay on the ground a few feet past the door.

"Why, you're all wet, Abigail," said her grandmother. "Didn't you think to bring an umbrella? It's been raining to end the world for the past few days."

Abigail stammered as Timothy ducked underneath the velvet rope, "I—I forgot."

"Well, you can take mine with you when you go. My old raincoat does quite well in weather like this. Of course, the cab picked me up in front of the apartment building, so I didn't have to walk to the bus stop like you did. Regardless . . ."

Timothy crawled into the dark administrative hallway. The book lay just out of reach. Beyond it was cold, unblinking darkness. Timothy was terrified to go any farther.

He could make out the cover—something about a corpse. The hallway seemed to close in as he inched forward, his fingers reaching the book.

"Timothy? What are you doing?"

He nearly screamed as he spun around to find Mr. Crane and one of the security guards standing in the doorway next to Abigail and her grandmother. He slid back underneath the velvet rope and struggled to rise, clutching the book behind his back. Slipping it underneath his shirt and into the lip of his pants, he said, "I dropped a penny."

"Please . . . come away from there," said Mr. Crane to Timothy, before noticing the stranger beside Abigail. "Are you . . . ? You're not a chaperone."

The old woman shook her head. "Thank you for letting me know."

"I'm sorry," said Mr. Crane, flustered.

"Please don't be," she replied. "I'm Abigail's grandmother. Zilpha Kindred. Funny coincidence meeting like this. If I'd remembered you were planning a trip to the museum, I would have tagged along for the ride. As it is, I took a cab. I have particular business to attend . . ." She glanced at Abigail, who seemed to have taken an interest in picking a piece of dirt out from underneath her fingernail. "Never mind. Carry on. Pretend I'm invisible."

Mr. Crane turned his attention to Timothy instead. "I think you've got some explaining to do, young man."

"Me?" said Timothy.

"You're lucky you didn't damage that beautiful painting upstairs. Throwing water like that. What could you possibly have been thinking?"

"But I didn't . . ."

"It wasn't Timothy, Mr. Crane," said Abigail quietly. "It was . . . someone else."

"Who?" said Mr. Crane.

The fire in Abigail's eyes seemed to spark at that. "Not Timothy!" Timothy felt a pang of triumph that she was standing up for him.

The teacher turned red, and his mouth dropped open.

"Abigail," whispered her grandmother. "Apologize right now."

She blushed but mumbled, "I'm sorry, Mr. Crane."

"This is not like you, Abigail," Zilpha said, placing a hand on her granddaughter's shoulder. She glanced harshly at Timothy, as if it was all his fault.

9.

Timothy and Abigail didn't tell Mr. Crane who threw the water balloon; they couldn't prove it.

After they had joined the rest of the class, Zilpha Kindred had kissed her granddaughter goodbye and quietly slipped back downstairs. Mr. Crane forced both Abigail and Timothy to accompany him, as the rest of the students were now free to roam and gather information regarding their projects. As they wandered, silently, Abigail had refused to glance up from the ground, lost once again in her own private world—a world where Timothy, apparently, was not allowed.

On the ride back to school, he sat by himself in the front of the bus, well away from both Stuart and Abigail. By then, he'd nearly dried off and was able to recall what had happened inside the museum. Timothy wondered if he'd momentarily gone bonkers, but he knew that couldn't be the case, not entirely. He had nearly forgotten the proof of the shadow man, which was currently pressed like a cold hand into the small of his back.

He pulled the book out from his pants. It was slight, the paper jacket was torn halfway down the back, and the entire bottom right corner was missing. On the cover was a simple painted illustration of a rosy-cheeked, dark-haired girl dressed in a calf-length blue skirt, socks pulled almost all the way up to her knees, a white sweater, and a red silk scarf wrapped around her thin neck. She knelt before the opening of a small dark hole that had been carved into the slope of a hill in a mossy forest. She looked over her shoulder curiously, as if she'd noticed someone creeping up behind her. In the background, silhouettes of several gothic buildings poked out from a hillside, looking like College Ridge up near Edgehill Road. Was this book a New Starkham story? Now Timothy was even more intrigued. He looked closer. The title stretched across the top of the book. *The Clue of the Incomplete Corpse: A Zelda Kite Mystery.* Someone named Ogden Kentwall had written the book.

Weird names. Weird book.

Timothy had the impression that the sight of the old woman had startled the shadow man, and in his haste to leave, he'd somehow dropped the book. Surely the man had meant to return and pick it up once everyone had gone. Too late, thought Timothy.

Unless he comes to take it back.

Goose bumps tickled Timothy's scalp. Maybe I should have left it there, he thought.

Quickly, he glanced over his shoulder, peering above the

heads of his classmates and out the rear window of the bus, trying to see through the mist and the rain to make out if there was a pair of headlights following close behind. There was nothing. He immediately turned and hunched his shoulders, trying to become invisible himself.

As the bus bumped back across the Taft Bridge toward New Starkham, Timothy opened the book's cover and began to read.

10.

By the time lunch ended back at school, Timothy had managed to get through the first couple of chapters. The story began with the description of an ordinary girl named Zelda Kite whose best friend, a fellow school newspaper reporter named Dolores Kaminski, had disappeared while on assignment at the local antiques shop. The mystery was simple, and the writing was fine, if not exactly literary like the stories Mrs. Medina made them read for English class. Timothy wondered what the man in the museum had been doing with an odd little book like this.

In fact, Timothy was so distracted by it, he didn't consider that Stuart Chen had neglected to sit with him at their usual table in the cafeteria. He also didn't notice the girl who regarded him curiously from the lunch line, her red hair finally lightening as it dried into stringy ringlets upon her hunched shoulders.

* * *

At the end of the day, Timothy was standing at his locker, leafing through the final few pages of the fifth chapter of *The Incomplete Corpse* when he came across a name written in the margins, scribbled in pencil just below the page number 102.

Carlton Quigley

At first, Timothy didn't even notice the writing. It had been written so lightly that it seemed almost ghostly compared to the text in the rest of the book. He held the pages like a flipbook, zipping through to the end in case there happened to be any more writing.

To his surprise, Timothy found two names further along. *Bucky Jenkins* stared at him from page 149 and *Leroy "Two Fingers" Fromm* from page 203, the second to last in the book.

Carlton Quigley. Bucky Jenkins. Leroy "Two Fingers" Fromm.

Timothy flipped from page 102 to 149, then 203, again and again, looking at the writing. Who were these people? he wondered. Why had someone written their names there?

Timothy grabbed his backpack. The faint scent of chlorine filled his nose as he unzipped it. That morning, somehow, he'd remembered to shove his swimsuit, goggles, and towel inside before leaving the house. Now he placed the strange new book on top of his swim gear and zipped up the bag.

Outside, to Timothy's surprise, he noticed Mrs. Chen's burgundy minivan waiting at the curb. Stuart sat in the front seat and actually waved at him. Timothy trudged down the stairs to the sidewalk. Stuart rolled down his window, and Mrs. Chen leaned past her son, obviously oblivious to the events of the day.

"Hi, Timothy!" she said. "Hurry up. Get in. Don't want to be late!" Timothy hesitated. "What are you waiting for?" she added.

"Yeah, what are you waiting for?" Stuart echoed her.

11.

Timothy meant to mention the water-balloon attack while still in the car, in front of Stuart's mother, but by the time they'd driven up the hill to the college's entrance, he realized that if he talked about what had happened at the museum, he might be forced to talk about why Stuart had done what he'd done in the first place. And if he mentioned the reason, he might be forced to mention some other things—things his parents had forbidden him mentioning, to Mrs. Chen especially. By the time the great gothic gymnasium appeared ahead, Timothy realized how much he wanted to talk about Ben with someone, *anyone,* who would listen.

But now, he wouldn't give Stuart the satisfaction, even if he apologized a million times.

Mrs. Chen pulled up to the curb in front of the main

entrance. Before Timothy was able to fully jump out of the vehicle, she called to him, "Please tell your mother I said hello."

"I will," Timothy answered, hiking his bag onto his shoulder.

"Timothy?" Mrs. Chen called. Stuart had already reached the top of the steps.

"Yeah?"

"She hasn't returned any of my messages lately. Is everything okay with her? How's Ben?"

She'd hit the nail on the head.

"I've gotta run, Mrs. Chen," he said. "Thanks for the ride!"

"O-Okay then," she said quietly. "See you boys after practice."

As Timothy entered the locker room, he realized he didn't want to be there. After everything that had happened that day, all he really wanted to do was curl up in bed and continue reading *The Clue of the Incomplete Corpse.* He was determined to find his own clue regarding the names written on pages 102, 149, and 203. Maybe the answer was in the story.

The locker room's dim lighting, high ceilings, and dark stone walls created a unique cryptlike atmosphere deep inside the building. Timothy found a spot in the farthest corner away from the showers, hidden at the end of the longest row of lockers. From his bag, he lifted away the mysterious book and carefully placed it onto the bench beside him.

“Let’s hustle, July,” called Coach Thom from the far end of the row. Clapping his hands and moving on, he shouted, “Water’s waiting, Chen. Move it.”

Timothy’s face burned. So much for hiding out now. He flung his bag into the nearest locker. He quickly changed into his bathing suit, before grabbing the book from the bench. Zelda Kite’s worried eyes glanced over Timothy’s shoulder, as if she knew that someone had crept up behind him.

Spinning around, Timothy was met with a smile by Stuart, standing inches away. Timothy nearly jumped but managed to control himself. “What do you want?” he said.

“Scare you?” said Stuart. “Sorry.”

“You didn’t scare me,” said Timothy. “I just didn’t expect you there.”

“Right.” Stuart briefly looked at the book in Timothy’s hands. “Pretty funny what happened today, don’t you think?”

Timothy shoved the book into his locker, snatched his towel off the floor, and wrapped it around his shoulders. “What was funny?”

“What happened to your partner,” said Stuart. “The water balloon?”

“How do *you* know it was a water balloon?” said Timothy, playing the game.

Stuart smiled. “Whatever, dude. We all thought it was pretty funny.”

“Well, I didn’t. I got pretty soaked.”

"Whose fault was that?"

Timothy shook his head. "Are you saying I threw the water balloon at myself?"

"No. I'm saying you were too close. You stand next to the target, you get wet."

"Stuart . . ." Timothy' face turned red. "You're such a . . . a fart-slap."

"A fart-slap?" said Stuart, laughing. "What the heck is a fart-slap?"

Timothy stared at the floor, thinking of Abigail's cleverness. "It's not good," he answered, then climbed over the bench and brushed past Stuart, heading for the showers.

12.

The water was cold. Swimming freestyle, Timothy stared at the ceramic tiles drifting away into the hazy deep end. When he reached the wall underneath the diving platforms, he noticed that Coach Thom was speaking with Stuart, two lanes over and a pool length away. Stuart sat on the water's edge in the shallow end. Their voices echoed throughout the large room.

"Where was it?" said Thom.

Stuart shook his head, closed his eyes, then pointed at the deep end. Thom peered into the water. "I've got a clear view of the entire bottom of the pool, Chen. I can assure you, I don't see any *monsters.* You want to get back in the water now?"

Monsters? Timothy chuckled before he ducked back under and pushed off the wall. What a freak! He'd heard a ton of excuses for wanting to sit out a lap or two, but that was the craziest in a very long time.

The weird thing, though, was that Stuart had looked truly scared. Timothy swept the bottom of the pool with his eyes, trying to make out exactly what Stuart could have mistaken for a monster. But there was nothing down there except for a couple of glimmering pieces of loose change, far away near the drain at the bottom of the twenty-five-foot well. Seconds later, he'd made it to the wall in the shallow end to find Stuart still sitting in the gutter, his feet pulled up out of the water.

Now Thom sounded really angry. "You can get in or go home, Chen. I'm not going to say it again. Let's move!"

Reluctantly, Stuart slid into the water. He glanced at Timothy briefly before popping his goggles over his eyes. He ducked under the lane lines and entered Timothy's lane. Timothy was about to push off the wall, when he felt Stuart grab his arm.

"What is it?" said Timothy.

Stuart's eyes were invisible behind his mirrored lenses. "It was the thing with the claw," he said in a low voice.

"*What* was the thing with the claw?"

"The monster from *Wraith Wars*?" said Stuart, sounding freaked out. "The game? It was at the bottom of the pool."

Timothy didn't even know how to respond. Hadn't they just been fighting? Obviously, Stuart was terrified. Timothy remembered how crazy he had felt in the basement of the museum that morning, when all the golden idols had stared at him.

"I didn't see anything down there," said Timothy. "Maybe your goggles were smudged."

Stuart nodded. "I'm gonna follow behind you, though, okay? In this lane."

Timothy sighed. "Okay."

When he finally pushed off the wall, he realized that, in a way, they'd both just apologized to each other.

Twenty laps later, Timothy hopped out of the pool to take a drink from the water fountain. He was out of breath and his brain was racing with numbers. Five hundred yards, twenty laps, twenty minutes on the clock . . .

Then, pages 102, 149, and 203.

And eventually names: Carlton Quigley. Bucky Jenkins. Leroy "Two Fingers" Fromm . . . Zelda Kite. Zilpha Kindred. Abigail Tremens.

Timothy had just come up from the fountain, when he noticed someone standing in the last row of bleachers. Since the lights hung low in a similar fashion to the locker room, the steep seats were dark. The pool itself was bright. Timothy held his hand up to shade the light.

What he saw sent goose bumps rippling across his skin. Timothy could see only a silhouette—the man in the long overcoat and the brimmed hat. He understood clearly why the man had come.

The book.

It was still in his locker.

The man descended the stadium stairs and slipped into the nearest exit, disappearing entirely into the shadows of the upstairs hallway.

Timothy turned and dashed toward the boys' lockers. Slipping and sliding on the cold ceramic tile, he heard Thom shout, "No running!" before careening through the doorway. He ignored his coach, fearing that, in his rush to get away from Stuart, he might have forgotten to put the padlock on his locker.

In the hallway, Timothy slowed. He suddenly felt foolish. Was he really willing to risk his life just to keep a stupid old kids' book?

He skidded to a halt. The hallway didn't look the same. It was longer than usual. Where had the showers gone?

Timothy turned around. The hallway behind him stretched on for what looked like hundreds of yards before disappearing into murky darkness.

Had he taken the wrong hallway? Maybe he was accidentally heading toward the girls' room? Something deep inside told him, *No*. He hadn't made a wrong turn—the hallway had.

Timothy decided to return to the pool, toward the safety

of his team, but as he ran, the hallway continued to grow even longer. The ceiling sank lower. The walls were covered with grime. The floor was slick with gray-green slime. Mildew. Or something. And it stank, like old cheese.

He stopped again. The pool entrance should have been directly in front of him. But all Timothy could see in both directions was the hallway, which was growing darker by the second. There were no pool sounds. No shouting, no splashing. He could almost hear the mold growing in the wall's crevices. The sound of his heart was pounding in his ears.

Timothy squeezed his eyes shut for a brief second and violently shook his head. Snap out of it, he told himself. When he opened his eyes again, he caught a glimpse of light at the end of the hallway behind him. Stainless steel. The showers! Timothy bolted. At least now, he knew where he was going.

He burst through the doorway into the shower room's yellow light. Beyond the showerheads was the cavernous locker room. He bounded to the last row of lockers. But when he peered around the rusted aluminum edge, the row was about half as long as usual. A T-shaped path veered where an L usually bent. Maybe he was remembering it wrong?

Without thinking, Timothy dashed forward, but when he reached the T, he knew for certain that the problem wasn't his memory.

His locker was not there.

Timothy glanced in both directions. The shadows were encroaching from the ceiling again, the low-hanging globes inching closer to the ground. How was that possible?

Though his mind raced, Timothy walked slowly, lightly, back toward the showers. His feet were cold, and his skin was prickly. He made his way to the end of the row and peeked around the corner, but the showers were no longer there. Instead, the sight of a dirty brick wall greeted him, like a slap in the face.

"No," Timothy groaned. He leaned against the locker at the end of the row. The coldness of the metal bit into his shoulder, and he leapt away from it, holding in a shriek.

A locker slammed. He jumped. He couldn't tell where the noise had come from.

Someone was with him, somewhere in this big room.

Timothy shivered. Then he ran. He wasn't sure where he was going. The more he ran, the more he realized he was not merely lost—the room didn't look familiar at all anymore. These lockers were bashed and battered, the doors hanging off their hinges. Some of them had been painted black; graffiti was scratched into their metal surfaces—words much worse than the one he'd called Stuart earlier—strange, almost alien symbols, horrific faces with slitlike feline eyes and gaping needle-filled mouths. Timothy tried not to think that anything could be hiding just inside these doors—Stuart's clawed monster, the Aztec idols, the cloudy creatures in the specimen jars. Things with black watchful eyes. The more Timothy ran, the more he realized that if he stopped, he'd regret it.

He came around a corner and screamed.

A man stood at the end of the corridor, his hand reaching into the nearest open locker. He turned to look at Timothy. The shadow from the brim of his hat obscured his face. His long gray overcoat hung almost all the way to the floor, barely covering his black wingtips. For a second, Timothy had the feeling he was staring at a ghost. Then the man withdrew from the locker. In his hand was the book; he used it to slam the locker shut.

Timothy was frozen with fear. He wanted to shout, *Put it down!* But the book didn't even belong to him. If anything, the man was simply stealing it back.

"You shouldn't take things that don't belong to you," said the man. His voice was low, resonant, a bit scratchy.

Timothy surprised himself by answering lamely, "I'm sorry."

"You had the chance to run at the museum this morning. Shoulda used it, Timothy. Leave her behind." The man was talking about Abigail. . . .

Slowly, the man raised his other hand—the one without the book—toward the ceiling. In this fist, he tightly gripped a different object. The two ends of a horseshoe jutted out from either side of the man's sleeve. A small piece of the object sparkled brightly as light from the nearest aluminum globe struck it. The overhead light grew fainter and fainter, until the locker room disappeared entirely.

Unable to see, Timothy tentatively reached out. Something pushed by him. He shouted and slammed himself against the nearest locker, flailing his arms for protection. After a few seconds, Timothy realized he was alone. He slowed his breathing, trying to calm down. I'm safe now, he told himself. Safe.

A moment later, the locker room appeared again. The lights were normal. The man was gone. Timothy stood at the end of the row where his own locker had been. Behind him, the yellow light from the shower room bled onto the concrete floor.

Timothy needed to get out of there. Beyond the showers, the crooked hallway revealed the way to the pool. But even that seemed too far away. Timothy turned and dashed around the corner, toward the gymnasium's lobby.

Once there, Timothy was flooded with relief. As several passing students stared at him, he realized he must look like a crazy person, standing there dripping in his wet bathing suit, eyes wild, out of breath. He didn't care.

Seconds later, from the direction of the pool, Timothy heard the sound of screaming.

13.

Timothy rushed past several of the college students who had wandered toward the pool entrance. Underneath the diving platforms, a group of people stood at the edge of the pool, raising a commotion. One of his teammates, a younger girl, was crying. In the water, the rest of the swim team held on to the lane lines. They had all stopped swimming and were paying attention to what was happening in the deep end.

Suddenly, Thom burst through the surface of the water from below. He was wearing all his clothes. He was holding someone in his arms. He kicked toward the edge of the pool, calling out for everyone to give him room. By the time Thom had reached the side, Timothy had managed to make his way through the crowd. That was when he realized who Thom was struggling to pull out of the water.

Stuart.

He was unconscious. His skin was a strange bluish color. Thom managed to lay Stuart out flat. He leaned toward Stuart's face, feeling for breath. After a couple seconds, Thom began pressing on Stuart's chest with both hands.

"What happened?" Timothy asked an older boy standing beside him.

"Not sure," said the boy. "The kid was down really deep. Thom thought he was fooling around, you know? He kept calling to him, but he wouldn't come up. So Thom jumped in."

The coach breathed into Stuart's mouth, then lifted his head. "Someone call an ambulance!" he shouted. He continued pressing on Stuart's chest. "And his parents!"

Timothy felt the same way he had in the locker room, when the rows of lockers seemed to have rearranged themselves. Lost. Was this really happening? Maybe this was all a dream—a nightmare like the one he'd had the night before about his brother. He closed his eyes and told himself to wake up. But when he opened his eyes, nothing changed.

Just then, Stuart shuddered. He coughed huge, wet, choking breaths. Timothy hugged himself.

Thank you, thank you, thank you, he thought to no one in particular.

THE HAUNTING OF ABIGAIL TREMENS

INTERLUDE

Wal-Mart Supercenter—Vero Beach, Florida

"Just let me know if you need a different size," said the salesgirl.

"I will," said the older woman, slipping into the dressing room and closing the door behind her.

Emma Huppert had needed a new bathing suit for years but hadn't wanted to shop for one until she'd lost a little weight. At her age, she found it harder than ever. Though finally this year, Emma had managed to stick with her resolution.

Emma adjusted the strap and examined herself in the mirror. The floral pattern was flattering, and the skirt that flirted out at the waist hid the parts that needed to be hidden. "Perfect," Emma whispered to herself. She lived so close to the beach but hadn't been in the water for at least a decade.

This would be a nice change. Something to do other than play bingo all day with the rest of the white-haired ladies in the retirement community.

The doorknob rattled, and Emma jumped. "There's someone in here!" she called over the door. She waited for an apology, but none came. "Rude," she whispered.

She and Bill had left Massachusetts almost twenty years

ago, but Florida never really felt like home. So many tourists always passing through. So many seasonal friends who came and went.

Emma often had to force herself to remember New Starkham. This bathing suit was her way of trying to get some of that feeling back, if only to swim in the same ocean she had when she'd been young. Not that all memories of her hometown were pleasant.

The doorknob rattled again, harder this time, as if someone was frantically trying to enter the dressing room. Emma nearly fell against the wall. "There is someone in here!" she called again, growing angry.

Probably just teenagers playing pranks, she imagined, catching her breath. Well, the bathing suit fit, so Emma decided to hurry up and let the pranksters tease someone else. When she bent down to pick up her blouse, someone slapped the door so hard that Emma yelped, leapt upright, and clutched her shirt to her chest. The slap came again and again and again. She could see under the door, but no one was standing outside.

Now Emma was frightened. She knew it wasn't the salesgirl doing this to her. She was almost certain that whoever was assaulting the door was no prankster either. For the past few weeks, she'd been seeing things she should not have been seeing. She'd managed to dismiss the other incidents as exhaustion, but this was not something she could ignore. She was trapped in a tiny room, wearing a bathing suit that did not yet belong to her. And outside was . . . well . . . No, that was impossible. There was no such thing as ghosts.

Emma reached for the doorknob. Grasping it, she turned her wrist slowly, then pulled the door open. Peeking out, she saw no one, so she swung the door wide.

But then, standing in the opposite cubicle, Emma noticed the girl. Her wet black hair was plastered to her dirty face, her brown skin pulled taut over her cheekbones. She wore the same stars-and-stripes dress she'd been wearing the last time Emma had seen her . . . nearly sixty years ago. "Delia," Emma croaked. Her sister.

The girl leapt across the aisle, arms raised, and Emma stumbled backward. *"It was your fault!"* screamed the girl. *"You weren't watching. You weren't watching. You weren't watching!"*

Emma hit the mirror behind her and covered her face. "I'm sorry!" she cried, sliding down the wall until she'd managed to curl herself into a ball on the carpet. "I'm so sorry, Delia! Please!" She felt someone grab at her shoulder. Emma slapped the hand away, then glanced up, expecting Delia to lean in at her with a mouthful of broken teeth.

Instead, the salesgirl stood over her, wearing a shocked expression. "Is everything all right, ma'am?"

Emma didn't know what to do. Lifting her eyes, she peered at the aisle outside the dressing room. No one else was there. She shook her head and wiped the tears from her eyes. "Everything is fine," Emma said, standing sturdily. She brushed herself off. "The bathing suit fits perfectly. I'll take it." The salesgirl nodded and stepped out of the cubicle.

Then a voice whispered from the adjacent dressing room, the same voice she'd been hearing for several weeks now, whenever she thought of her sister. It said, *Your fault . . .*

"Wait!" Emma grabbed the salesgirl's arm. The girl looked worried. "Can you do me a favor?" Emma asked. "Just . . . stand outside the door? Make sure no one tries to come in?"

The salesgirl simply stared back, as if Emma had lost her mind.

14.

The morning after swim practice, the clouds had broken, and bits of blue shone through the gray. After he got off the bus, Timothy went directly to the school library. There were only ten minutes before the first bell, but there was something he needed to do. He plopped himself down at an empty computer, logged on to the Internet, and did a search of the name Ogden Kentwall.

The first few pages of results didn't produce any exact matches—a few "Ogden"s, several "Kentwall"s, but nothing else. Just when Timothy was about to give up and head to his locker, he finally came across a Web site for an independent bookstore, called The Enigmatic Manuscript, located in the northwest corner of the state. The Web site listed several other Zelda Kite Mysteries and a brief biography of the author, which had been written by the owner of the store, a woman named Frances May.

"Ogden Kentwall is actually a pseudonym for a man whose real name was Hieronymus Kindred," wrote Frances, "a lawyer from Boston, who allegedly based the character of Zelda Kite on his teenaged niece. Kindred's foray into children's literature was short-lived, due to the series' never

really catching on. His three titles that survive, however, have a strange, subtle charm, and I would not be surprised if someday they are rediscovered by young audiences. I have one copy of each, available for purchase through this site. . . ."

As Timothy read the short blurb, he began to feel a chill. Hieronymus Kindred? Why did the name sound familiar? Before he had a chance to think about it, the first bell rang. Timothy quickly logged off the computer, snatched his bag from the desk, and headed toward homeroom.

By the time Timothy made it to Mr. Crane's third-period class, the school was buzzing about Stuart. Timothy hadn't said anything about what had happened the night before, yet everyone was looking at him strangely, expectant, as if he might know something more. He sat down and tried not to look at the empty chair to his left.

Before Mr. Crane came through the door, Brian Friedman and Randy Weiss had mentioned Stuart's name. Timothy wouldn't have listened to them, except that he knew Randy's mother was a nurse in New Starkham Hospital's emergency room.

"I overheard my parents last night," Randy began. "Supposedly, when they brought Stuart in, he was talking really weird."

"Weird how?" said Brian.

"I think I heard my mom say he thought"—Randy paused—"well . . . some sort of . . . *monster* tried to drown him."

"Maybe you heard her wrong."

"Yeah . . . maybe. I don't think she wanted me listening. So did you start the history project yet?"

Timothy held his face in his hands. Something strange was going on here. Randy's story was an echo of Stuart's claims from the side of the pool last night.

Out of the corner of his eye, Timothy noticed Abigail slinking down the aisle toward her desk in the back of the classroom. Her eyes were puffy. She looked as though she hadn't slept at all the night before either.

Moments later, Mr. Crane entered. He too looked strange. His button-down shirt was a little wrinkled and his swollen eyes looked worried and anxious, like he wanted the period to be over as quickly as possible.

Mr. Crane began the class by asking the students which artifact from the museum each pair had chosen for their project. Timothy listened as his classmates rattled off their answers. Distracted, Mr. Crane kept glancing at the shelves where the glass specimen jars sat.

Suddenly, Timothy realized something. Mr. Crane had been in the basement of the museum too, just after Timothy had seen the golden idols stare at him. If Timothy had seen some strange things the night before, and Abigail looked like she hadn't slept as well, maybe something had happened to all of them down there? Something that was keeping them up at night. Making them *see things*. Just like Stuart.

Timothy heard Abigail call out their chosen artifact from the back of the room. "The *Edge of Doom* painting," she said. Mr. Crane half-smiled and moved on to Kimberly Mitchell. But Timothy kept looking at Abigail. Her grandmother had been in the basement with them as well. He wondered if she had been seeing things since then too.

The old woman had a strange name, didn't she? What was it again? It had been stuck in Timothy's brain all night long, but now he couldn't seem to grasp it. "Z" something. Zelda?

No. Not Zelda.

Zilpha.

Zilpha Kindred.

Timothy felt a jolt rush through his body, and he dropped his pencil on the floor. Scrambling to pick it up again, he only kicked it farther into the aisle.

Kindred, he thought. Her last name is Kindred, like the author of *The Clue of the Incomplete Corpse*.

Obviously, here was the connection. But what did it mean? Could Abigail's grandmother possibly have something to do with what had happened at the museum yesterday morning and at the gymnasium last night?

"Okay," said Mr. Crane. "We've had enough fun for now." The class collectively groaned. "Please open your textbooks to chapter seven." On the board, he wrote *Pre-Colonial America.*

Timothy tore a piece of paper from his notebook. He quickly jotted a note, folded it up, and turned toward Abigail. He dropped the folded paper on the floor and swiftly kicked it in Abigail's direction.

Before she had a chance to lean over and pick it up, Mr. Crane said, "Mr. July, would you please bring that to the front of the class?"

As Timothy stood up, his stomach felt like it was filled with a big chunk of ice. Abigail bent over and picked up the note. With a surprising look of pity, she handed it to him.

Mr. Crane folded his arms across his chest. "Well?"

Reluctantly, Timothy stepped forward to the large desk in front of the long green chalkboard. "What has come over you these past couple days?" the teacher whispered.

Timothy could feel the eyes of his class whispering across his back. "Dunno," he mumbled.

"Go on, then." Mr. Crane nodded at the note in Timothy's hand. "Let's hear it."

Timothy knew he could just make something up, but if Mr. Crane saw the writing from over his shoulder, everything would be worse, because then the class would know he'd been lying. "Abigail, Ireallyneedtotalktoyouaboutyourgrandmother."

"Ah-ah-ah, Mr. July," said Mr. Crane. "Slow down. We couldn't hear you. Again, please."

Red-faced, Timothy read the note again, this time so everyone could hear. "Abigail, I really need to talk to you about your grandmother."

The laughter was immediate and overwhelming.

Mr. Crane said, "I've got a little project for you. Meet me after school, Mr. July. No later than five minutes past the last bell. Right here." He glanced nervously at the shelves again. "Now, class, chapter seven . . ."

Ashamed, Timothy slipped into his seat. Seconds later, from the corner of the room, he could feel Abigail Tremens looking at him. He couldn't bring himself to look back.

15.

Timothy sleepwalked through the rest of the day. He was standing at his locker, just after the last bell had rung, wondering what project Mr. Crane had in mind for his detention, when he felt a hand on his shoulder. He jumped and spun around, embarrassed.

Abigail was standing behind him. "Sorry about what happened with that note," she said. "I wasn't quick enough."

"S'okay," said Timothy. "I only came up with the idea to eat it after I'd read it in front of the whole stupid class."

To his surprise, Abigail laughed. "Oh my God, I would've *paid* to see you do that."

Timothy shrugged. "Next time, then."

She laughed again, but a second later, her face quickly changed. "So . . . um . . . what was that about my grandmother?"

She drew her eyebrows close together and somehow managed to repossess that ability to look inside him.

"I—I . . . ," Timothy stammered, trying to finish his sentence. "I'm going to be late."

"Late for what?"

"For my detention with Mr. Crane."

"We could talk after your detention. I'm staying in my grandmother's apartment for a while. You could, like, come over if you want?"

"I could do that. Sure."

"Good," said Abigail. "I could actually use your help with something."

"Really? With what?"

She shook her head. "It's sort of complicated."

On a scrap of paper, Abigail quickly wrote down her grandmother's address and handed it to him.

Mr. Crane was waiting for Timothy, leaning against the chalkboard, staring at the side wall. He barely glanced at Timothy as he came through the door. "You're late," he said.

"Sorry," Timothy answered. His teacher continued to stare at the shelves on the side of the room. The specimen jars rested there, silent and unassuming as always. "Uh, Mr. Crane," Timothy said, "what do you want me to do?"

Mr. Crane finally turned to look at him, pulled away from the sight of the specimens, as if from a dream. "I . . ."

He cleared his throat. "I need you to take those jars out of here."

Timothy flinched. "Where do you want me to take them?"

"I don't care," said Mr. Crane. "They don't belong in this classroom. I don't know why they've lasted as long as they have." He pointed out the window. "Take them outside to the Dumpster," he said, slipping into his corduroy jacket. He clutched his leather briefcase under his arm. "Just close the door when you're done."

"Wait a second," said Timothy. "You're leaving?"

Mr. Crane wiped his forehead with the back of his hand. "I'm sorry, Timothy. I haven't been feeling well. I trust you'll be fine alone." He headed toward the door.

Before his teacher slipped away entirely, Timothy looked at the specimen jars one more time. "Mr. Crane?" he said.

The teacher stopped in the doorway, but he didn't turn around. "Yes, Timothy?" he answered stiffly.

"Why do you really want to get rid of the jars?"

"I'm sorry?"

"Why *now*?"

Mr. Crane turned around. His eyes were wide with some sort of secret. "Why now? I told you, they do not belong here."

Timothy remembered the black eyeball he'd seen two days ago, staring at him through the dusty glass. Staring or dead—it had been impossible to tell the difference at the time.

"Did you see something?" said Timothy, almost a whisper.

"Excuse me?"

"In the jars. Did you *see* something?" This time, he said it more loudly.

"See something? Like what?"

"I don't know. Something scary."

The teacher opened his mouth to speak, but all that came

out was a harsh crackling sound.

After Mr. Crane was gone, Timothy dragged the closest desk toward the wall. He climbed on top of it and, shuddering, removed the specimens from the shelves.

In the closet behind Mr. Crane's desk, Timothy found an empty cardboard box. Working quickly, he placed the jars in the box, looking away every time he found a specimen that was especially heavy or clearly visible through the liquid.

Something in these jars had scared Mr. Crane yesterday. What had he seen?

There was a connection between all of these events. Too many pieces of this strange puzzle had matching edges.

The box was full. Every jar fit inside. Straining, Timothy lifted the box and headed to the parking lot. Outside, the garbage bin was as high as Timothy was tall. The lid was open, but as Timothy stood there, he realized that he couldn't toss the box inside. As disgusting as some of these creatures appeared to be, he felt weird throwing them in the garbage.

Besides, the box was simply too heavy. Timothy placed it on the ground, then quickly made the sign of the cross. "May you rest in peace," he whispered. It seemed right.

With a nod, he turned away and headed toward the address Abigail had scrawled on the piece of paper in his pocket.

16.

The apartment building was sixteen stories tall—the tallest building in the neighborhood. Made of pale blond stone, it stood on the crest of Shutter Avenue, south of the bridge.

Timothy slowly made his way through the front garden, staring up at the building. Lots of windows. Lots of curtains. The front doors were made of black iron lace. Inlaid into the stone over the entrance were dark marble words: THE MAYFAIR. As Timothy reached out to take the handle, the door swung inward. A man stood just inside the lobby. "*Mi amigo,* who are you here to see?"

"Umm . . . I'm here for Abigail."

"Abigail?"

"She's uh . . . staying with her grandmother? Mrs. Kindred?"

* * *

He was delivered by the elevator to a small hallway with three large black doors, one of which was marked 16B. Abigail's place.

As he approached, he heard a dog barking. Then came Abigail's voice: "Hepzibah! No!" Footsteps. The doorknob turned, and there she was, wearing a sad smile and an oversized blue artist smock. At her feet, a small gray dog greeted him, loudly. Timothy bent down to say hello, but the dog backed away into the apartment's foyer. "Just ignore her. She thinks she runs the place," said Abigail, glancing at the dog. "Don't you, little queen?" Hepzibah listened for a second, then began barking again. Abigail rolled her eyes. "You don't have to stand in the hallway," she said to Timothy. "She won't bite."

"Oh, that's not what I'm afraid of."

Abigail raised an eyebrow. "What *are* you afraid of, then?"

Timothy felt his face flush. He stammered, "Th-that came out wrong. I meant . . . I'm not afraid of your dog. That's all." He came through the door. "Hepzibah? Strange name. Where'd you come up with it?"

"I didn't come up with it. My grandmother loves Nathaniel Hawthorne. Hepzibah's a character in one of his books," Abigail said. The dog sniffed Timothy's cuff. He stuck out his palm. Hepzibah considered him, then gave several soft kisses. "See? She likes you."

"Good. I like her too." Looking around, Timothy felt

small. "Cool place. It's huge." Across the foyer, a wide arched entry opened into a sprawling living room filled with antique furniture. Outside, through paneled French doors, was an enormous roof patio. Several of the spires from the college were visible beyond the railing, and beyond those were the river and then the hills of Rhode Island. Through a smaller doorway in the foyer, a long hallway stretched into darkness.

"Yeah, I guess it's okay," said Abigail.

"You don't like it?"

"Well, *I* didn't ask to live here." Suddenly, she looked at him, her eyes wide. "Oh my God, I probably sound like such a little brat. I'm sorry."

"No, you don't."

"My grandmother is really lucky to have this place. And I'm really lucky to be able to stay until . . . well, for now. It's just that at night . . . it can get a little . . . creepy."

"Creepy how?" said Timothy, suddenly noticing the many shadows in the numerous corners.

"Here," said Abigail, leading him into the dining room, changing the subject. "You can put your stuff down. I've already gotten started in the kitchen."

"Started with what?"

She turned to look at him. With an embarrassed smile, she said, "You'll see."

Timothy dropped his coat and bag on a chair at the end of the dining table, then followed Abigail through a series of doors to a narrow, cluttered kitchen. The countertop was scattered with a number of plastic bottles, and on the stove sat a small cardboard box. On the cover, a woman smiled as she ran her hands through her black hair. The words *COLOR ME WILD—RAVEN SILK* leapt out in white text underneath the woman's shapely chin.

"You're going to dye your hair black?"

"Nope," said Abigail, snatching the box from the stovetop and handing it to him. "You're going to do it for me."

Hepzibah came around the corner from the direction of the dining room. She sat in the doorway and looked at him, as if prepared to watch the show.

"You want me to *dye your hair*?" asked Timothy, appalled.

"You don't need to be good." She sighed and rolled her eyes. "I just need an extra pair of hands to get the back, but the box only comes with one pair of gloves, so you might as well just do the whole thing. You don't really mind, do you?"

Timothy thought about that. After everything that he'd been through that week, helping his new friend dye her hair shouldn't be a big deal.

His new friend? Was that what they were now?

"Okay," said Timothy softly.

"Great." Abigail reached into the open box and pulled out a pair of plastic gloves. "See if these fit. I'll start mixing."

Hepzibah followed as they set themselves up at the long dining room table. Abigail spread out some old newspapers underneath their supplies, then sat in one of the high-backed chairs. Grabbing the plastic bottle, which Abigail had filled with pungent-smelling chemicals, Timothy squeezed a lavender-colored gel onto her head.

"Ooh, it feels gross!" she said.

"Sorry," said Timothy.

He remembered the reason he'd come here: to talk to

Abigail about her grandmother. But he still didn't know how to tell his story.

"Why did you want to do this anyway?" he said instead.

"I guess I just want to be someone else for a change. I'm cutting it all off next."

"Really? All of it? Like a crew cut?"

"Nah, sort of, like . . . ear length. I've got the scissors in the bathroom." She glanced up at him. "Make sure you get it all even. Then just start combing it through."

Even through the gloves, the gel was squishy. "Is it just you and your grandmother here?" he asked.

"No. I came with my mom from New Jersey when Gramma fell again last month. Mom thinks she's getting sick. I just think she's getting old and doesn't want to admit it. She says to my mom, 'If I'm sick, you're sick.' "

"*Is* your mother sick?"

"Not in the conventional sense of the word." Abigail suddenly burst out laughing. "My mother suffers from a disorder called *Freakazoidism*."

Despite all the talk of illness, or perhaps because of it, Timothy couldn't hold back his own laughter. "So do *my* parents!" he said.

"Yeah," said Abigail. "My mom left my dad . . . like, *left*-left him, and didn't tell me, and thought I wouldn't notice that they weren't living together anymore, you know? In the same state?"

"But I thought you came here to help your grandmother."

Abigail raised her eyebrows and shook her head. "There's always an ulterior motive with my mom. She really just needed a place to go. *Voilà*—New Starkham, here we come!"

"Wow," said Timothy. "That's harsh."

"That's the truth. The funniest thing is that she thinks she has me fooled, that I'm just so young and gullible." She sniffed. "So why are your parents freaks?"

"They're not freaks, exactly. They just don't really seem to know how to talk to me." Abigail didn't say anything. Before he knew it, he blurted out, "My brother's unit was attacked overseas. He got hurt. Bad. They're keeping him in a coma, I think to protect his brain."

Abigail shuddered and brought her hand to her mouth. "He's in the—what, the army?" she asked. Timothy nodded. She grabbed his hand, and he flinched. "I'm so sorry . . . I had no idea."

"No—it's—" Timothy stammered. "Nobody did. That's the thing . . . My parents didn't want me to tell anyone."

"Why not? It's public information anyway. Isn't it?"

"I don't know. I think they felt ashamed. Like his injury is their fault. They don't want their friends to blame them."

"*That alone* is ridiculous, but what on earth does that have to do with *you*?"

"What do you mean?"

"Haven't they thought that you might want to, I dunno, talk about it with someone?"

Timothy shook his head. "Guess not."

"I mean, ever since I moved here, all I've wanted to do is talk to my cousins back in Jersey about everything that's happening. It's good that they listen on the phone, you know, about Gramma, and Mom and Dad, but still, there are things I feel like I can't tell anyone . . . not even them . . . and it's kinda driving me crazy." Abigail blinked, as if she expected him to ponder that last statement. "So I sort of know what you've been going through."

"Thanks," said Timothy, secretly wondering what it was that she couldn't tell anyone. Would she tell him now?

"So where is your brother?"

Guess not. "He's in a military hospital somewhere in Germany. He's been . . . critical for a while now. They say they'll send him home when he's healthy enough to travel, even if he *is* unconscious," said Timothy. Abigail was staring at him again. Her head was slick with purple goo. She looked funny. He smiled. After a few seconds, he realized that he'd actually finally told someone about his brother. It had been easier than he thought it would be. "So . . . what is it that *you* can't tell anyone?"

Abigail glanced at the floor, her mouth pursed. She actually looked like she was considering the answer, but then said, "Never mind. It's not important."

17.

After they cleaned up, Abigail put on a plastic bathing cap and led Timothy down the long hallway to a small room. The dark purple walls were entirely covered with black-and-white photographs in black wooden frames.

"My grandmother was a photographer for a local newspaper. Sometimes she wrote, but mostly she just took pictures." She pointed at one picture that looked like flowers of light, blossoming in the night sky. "The Fourth of July. Cool, huh?"

Timothy nodded.

Against the far wall was a twin-sized brass trundle bed. They plopped down on the mattress, giggling at the way she looked. Hepzibah leapt onto the bed too, circled a small spot in the corner several times, then lay down.

"Do you want to listen to some music?" said Abigail. In the corner of the room was a low bookcase, on top of which sat an old record player. The shelves below it contained vinyl records.

"Okay."

"They belonged to my grandfather before he died. Gramma said I could have 'em. Pick out whatever you want," said Abigail. "We've got a half hour before rinse time."

Timothy slid off the bed. Abigail followed. The record jackets were old and dusty. They'd been arranged in alphabetical order. Lots of country music. Not his favorite—but some of the covers looked interesting. He plucked a record from the shelf. *"Gunfighter Ballads,"* Timothy read. "Cool title." He handed it to Abigail. She slipped the disk from its envelope, placed it on the turntable, then lifted the needle. A dark melody began to play.

"So," said Abigail, sitting down on the bed again. "Now you know that my grandmother was a photographer. What else did you want to know?"

"It's not that simple," he said. She stared at him, curious. "I mean . . . I need to tell you something first. But I don't know where to start."

Abigail settled against the wall and folded her hands in her lap, as if preparing for a bedtime story. "It's always best to start at the beginning."

* * *

By the time the needle reached the center of the record, Timothy had said everything he'd meant to say. The book, the names, the author. The locker room. Stuart's monster. For the most part, while he spoke, Abigail listened intently, barely reacting when he got to the most outrageous and unbelievable parts of the story. Now she stared at the patchwork quilt underneath her. Her eyes were wide, her mouth pressed tight.

After nearly five seconds of silence, Timothy couldn't take it anymore.

"What do you think?" he said. "Am I crazy?"

Leaning forward, Abigail reached into her back pocket. She pulled out her silver lighter, flipped open the lid, and brushed her finger against the flint wheel. Flame bloomed in her fist. She stared at it for a few seconds, then said, "If you're crazy, then I'm crazy too." What was that supposed to mean?

The flame wicking at the tip of the lighter was hypnotic. "Have you ever seen anything like what I've seen?" he said.

To his surprise, Abigail clicked the lighter closed, squeezed her eyes shut, then nodded quickly. But before he could even respond, she exclaimed, "Shoot! I have to rinse this junk out of my hair." She slid off the bed and raced toward the door. Hepzibah woke up, gave a short bark, and chased her out of the room. A moment later, Timothy followed.

In the bathroom, Abigail had her head underneath the bathtub faucet. When she turned the water off, Timothy asked, "Do you think your gramma has something to do with all of this?" She ignored him, hiding underneath a towel, using it to rub her head dry. "Abigail," Timothy began again, speaking slowly so she could understand the importance of what he was saying, "I can't shake this feeling that something terrible is about to happen. I need to do something about it. If you know something, please . . . tell me."

She stopped drying her hair. Finally, she pulled the towel away. For a brief moment, Timothy thought he was looking at a brand-new person, someone he'd never met before. Her hair was purple-black. It completely obscured her face, like a ghost in a scary movie, and when she brushed her hair to the side, she didn't look at him. "Wait here," she said. "I'll be back."

A few seconds later, she returned. She showed him a Polaroid picture of her bedroom. "Have you ever heard of an author named Nathaniel Olmstead?"

"Yeah," said Timothy, unsure what the author had to do with the Polaroid. "I've read some of his books. Totally creepy."

"I used to be obsessed with them. My favorite was *The Revenge of the Nightmarys.*"

"I didn't read that one."

"It was about this gang of evil ghost girls. The book was so popular, they came out with trading cards. I collected them all."

"I saw those once at the comic-book store with Stuart," said Timothy, handing the photo back to Abigail. Suddenly, Timothy felt guilty, like he should be at the hospital. "I think he actually bought a pack. What do they have to do with anything?"

She plopped herself down on the edge of the bathtub and pulled the lighter out of her pocket. She lit it. "My father's lighter," she said. "I wanted him to stop smoking, so I stole it from him before we left New Jersey. I didn't actually think it would change anything. Fire is one of the easiest things in the world to find. I guess it was more of a symbolic gesture?" The flame flickered as she breathed on it. "Like, if he realized that I was the one who took it from him, he might know that I still think about him every day, and even though we don't see each other anymore, the fact that I stole it would matter to him so much that he would stop smoking altogether. . . . Stupid." She held the flame underneath the Polaroid. The paper slowly caught fire. "The funny thing is, he hasn't mentioned that it's missing." She tossed the photograph into the bathtub behind her, where it curled up, black and dead. Seconds later, the flame fizzled out in a hiss of weak smoke.

Abigail finally looked up again. Her newly black hair

hung down at either side of her face. Her eyes seemed to change, to sharpen. She smiled, and whispered, "I'm such an idiot." She waited a moment, then, as if an afterthought, hitched a quick breath and added, "I thought I could hide."

That last sentence gave Timothy chills. "Hide?" he said. "From who?"

"That's the real reason I dyed my hair."

"You dyed your hair to hide from your father?"

"No, Timothy. I'm telling you something else now. You told me, and now *I'm* telling you."

"Telling me what?"

"About the Nightmarys."

18.

Growing up in Clifton, New Jersey, Abigail Tremens actually had friends—not many, but enough to keep busy after school.

Things changed the summer before sixth grade, when two new girls moved into Abigail's neighborhood. They both happened to be named Mary. Oddly, Mary Brown was white, and Mary White was black; they were both beautiful. The two Marys formed an immediate bond. They liked the same music and food and clothes. They seemed to know each other's thoughts. Abigail had never shared anything quite like it with any of her friends, and she wondered what it might feel like to be that close with someone.

At the beginning of September that year, the two Marys began to make their mark at Clifton Middle School. For some reason, they ignored Abigail. Unfortunately, the girls in her class listened when the Marys spoke. The boys with whom Abigail usually played games after school stopped inviting her to join in. Abigail began to feel as invisible as air. Soon she was sitting by herself at lunch and walking home from school alone. Together, the Marys were an *entity,* the likes of which Abigail had never seen before. She didn't like it, and she decided she didn't like *them.* So Abigail gave them a taste of their own medicine.

She made up a nasty name for the two girls: the Nightmarys, of course. To Abigail's horror, the girls liked it, and it stuck. They wore it like a badge of honor. Abigail quickly grew tired of the nickname. *The Nightmarys request your attention during lunch period,* Janet Holm had told Harriet Lincoln during English class. *The Nightmarys told me I look pretty today,* Beth Reid cooed to herself in the bathroom mirror. *The Nightmarys told me to tell you that they're having a party, and you're not invited,* Mike Swenson had cruelly informed Abigail one Friday afternoon. She'd gone home in tears.

In March of the next year, Abigail learned that she and her mother would leave Clifton for New Starkham. When they arrived at her new home, Abigail realized that she had finally managed to get away from the Nightmarys—something she had wished for the past two years. Despite everything else, she was happy about that.

✲ ✲ ✲

She had been at Paul Revere Middle School for a week when it started.

One night, while finishing her homework in her bedroom, Abigail saw movement through her window. A blur of white. Outside was a stretch of patio. Something had crossed it. Abigail bolted upright on her mattress. After a few moments of quiet, she dismissed the movement as a seagull. There were plenty of those in New Starkham.

But the next night, it happened again. A little after midnight, she awoke to a soft tapping on glass. Before she even opened her eyes, Abigail feared what she would see at the window—two faces, smiling at her. Instead of looking, Abigail crawled out of bed, shielding her eyes as she made her way to the hallway. She shuffled to her grandmother's bedroom and slipped under the covers next to her.

Over a bowl of cereal, it was easier to toss off these occurrences as being influenced by the dark and the unfamiliar. Her mind was playing tricks on her. She was only nervous that there were "Nightmarys" at her new school. Things would work themselves out if she continued to be invisible, something she was already good at. At school during the day, she stayed by herself, tried to be inconspicuous. At night, she tucked her blanket over her head.

It worked . . . until the night she awoke to find the two girls standing in the corner of her room near the record player. This time, she could see them much more clearly. They looked like the girls from Clifton, but they were also different, as if half sisters with the creatures from the Nightmarys trading-card collection. Their hair hung limply from their heads. Their feet were bare. They wore matching dirty white lace dresses, which hung from their thin bodies like sacks. Abigail cringed in her bed, too frightened now to even make a sound. The spot where their faces should have been was simply blurry, like a shot of fast motion caught on still film. When Abigail stared too long, she saw things in the blur—things that should not have existed in place of their eyes, nose, and mouth—things too disturbing for her to later recall.

"Don't shout," said one. Mary Brown's voice.

"We want to be your friends," said the other. Mary White.

"I—I," Abigail managed to stammer, trying to keep them at bay. "I don't want any friends. Please, leave me alone."

The girls laughed as they stepped forward. "But we're lonely," said Mary White.

"Remember what that feels like, Abigail?" said Mary Brown. "Come play our game." Their voices were hypnotizing.

"But it's the middle of the night. My mom would hear."

"We'll take care of your mother . . . and your grandmother." The way the girls spoke snapped Abigail wide awake.

She grabbed a book she'd been reading before bed from the nightstand. "Stay away from them," she shouted, and threw the book at the descending shadows. When the book hit the far wall with a thump, Abigail realized that the girls were no longer there. She quickly turned on the bedside lamp and filled the darkness with light.

Since then, Abigail slept with the lights on. This, however, did not stop the girls from coming back. Again and again. Begging her to follow them into the night. To play their game. To be their friend.

19.

Abigail continued to sit on the edge of the bathtub, flicking the lighter on and off. Her hair hung in front of her face. It was nearly dry now.

Timothy felt a chill as he leaned against the sink.

"Do you think *I'm* crazy?" Abigail said. Timothy shook his head. She pointed at the crumpled black paper in the bathtub. "I took that picture last night, with Gramma's camera. The black smudge was where the girls were standing."

"I didn't see a smudge," said Timothy. "I just saw your bedroom."

"It was right in the center," said Abigail. "They were there!" She looked at the ash in the tub, as if she now wished she hadn't burned the photograph.

"I . . . believe you," said Timothy, smiling weakly. "There's got to be a connection between your story and mine. If we're both not crazy, then someone or something out there is trying to make us feel like we are."

"I know the connection."

"You do?"

She nodded. "It's you."

"Me?" he said, his voice rising.

Abigail closed the lighter and slipped it into her pocket.

"Partly." All the color had faded from her face. "Last night, the girls knew about what happened at the museum. You know, with the water balloon? They knew I was angry at Stuart for throwing it. And at Mr. Crane for allowing it to happen. And at . . . well . . . you."

"Me? What did I do?" Timothy asked.

"I can't even remember now." She blushed. "They said they had helped me. I didn't understand, and they said that soon I would. They said that since they'd helped me, I should go with them. Play their game. That I *owed* them." She was silent for a few seconds. "I didn't know what to say. I mean, how do you argue with a couple of . . . whatever they are."

"You're *not* going anywhere with them."

"Of course not. I didn't agree to anything."

"They said that they helped you. How?"

Abigail shrugged, unsure. "Horrible things happened to the three of you."

"The three of who?"

"Stuart. You. And Mr. Crane."

"I don't understand."

Abigail sighed. "The Nightmarys *helped* me. What happened to the three of you, happened *because* of me. You saw that creepy man. Stuart saw the monster in the pool."

Timothy blinked. "And Mr. Crane saw something scary in those jars."

"In Nathaniel Olmstead's book," said Abigail, "the Nightmarys have the power to frighten people. To make monsters. *My* Nightmarys made you see what you saw. Even though I didn't ask for it, the Nightmarys 'helped' me. And almost killed Stuart along the way." Her voice wavered. "When I found out what happened to him, I knew it was my fault. I never wanted anyone to get hurt. Or scared, even. I just wanted to be left alone."

"Maybe there *are* no Nightmarys. Maybe *you* have the power to frighten people," said Timothy, feeling almost foolish. "Maybe, like, deep down, you were really angry at all of us. So, like, unconsciously or something, you made us all see things . . . things that weren't really there."

"I wouldn't do that." Abigail shook her head. "I *couldn't* do that."

"Say you could . . . maybe you didn't *mean* to."

"But Stuart ended up in the hospital. If there was *nothing* there, if he was just seeing things, how did he get hurt?"

Timothy shook his head. "He *believed* he saw a monster. He got scared and inhaled some water."

"No," said Abigail, pressing her palms to her temples. "I can't believe that I did that. I mean, yeah, I was angry at him, but I never wanted any of this to happen."

"But—"

"No, Timothy. I know I'm right. I'm not anything like that. At first I actually had the same thought." She smiled weakly. "But now I know this is about something else."

"How do you know?"

"There are too many other things involved that don't add up."

"Like what?"

"Like . . . that book you found. And the names that were written in it. And, I suppose, most importantly . . . that it might be about my grandmother."

Timothy considered that.

"This goes beyond me and my stupid problems," said Abigail. She grabbed a chunk of her hair and waved it at him. "I mean, before you told me your story, I *actually* thought I could hide from them. I dyed my hair. I was planning on sleeping on the couch in the living room tonight. I thought maybe they wouldn't recognize me, and then tomorrow . . ."

"Tomorrow, what?" said Timothy.

"Tomorrow, I was going to take a bus back to New Jersey. My dad's waiting for me there."

"Oh . . ." Timothy felt as though she'd sucker punched

him. He realized how much he didn't want to go through this alone.

"But I can't do that anymore. Not now that you're involved," she said simply.

Timothy nodded, relieved. "I think the most important thing for us to figure out is who this man is—the one I keep seeing. And the book. If they're both real, not created, like you said, by . . . the Nightmarys, they might be the key to what is actually going on here."

Down the hall, a doorknob rattled. They both jumped.

Abigail leapt from the tub and closed the bathroom door. She opened the mirror cabinet and grabbed a pair of big black scissors.

20.

"Abigail? Honey? Are you home?" a sweet, high voice called from the foyer.

Chunks of her hair rained down upon the floor. Abigail tossed the scissors into the sink and turned around. Her hair now lay in jagged chunks just below her ears, swooping up even shorter in the back.

"How do I look?" Abigail whispered, a smile in her eyes.

"Uh . . . different," Timothy managed to say. He couldn't believe she'd just chopped off her hair like that.

"Perfect."

"Abigail?" The voice had come halfway down the hall.

"I'm in the bathroom," Abigail called back. Then she whispered to Timothy, "Now's your chance."

"Chance for what?"

"To ask my grandmother about the book."

"But—"

Abigail threw the door open and leapt into the hallway. Her mother screamed, then gasped.

"Abigail? Is that you? What have you done to yourself?"

"You don't like it?"

"To be perfectly honest," her mother answered dramatically, "no, I do not like it."

Timothy cowered in the bathroom. This was happening too fast. What if Abigail's grandmother freaked out when he asked her about the book? He looked over his shoulder for a way to escape, but all he could see was a tiny pane of fogged glass.

"Mother!" Abigail's own mother cried. "Come look what Abigail's done to herself!"

Abigail peeked at Timothy from around the doorframe and waved. "Come on," she said. Timothy reluctantly followed her down the hall, his heart in his throat. Suddenly, a hunched silhouette shuffled in front of them. They froze where they stood.

"Oh!" the old woman cried. "Abigail, you frightened me." Mrs. Kindred contemplated the two of them for several seconds, then said, "For a moment, I thought I was looking into a mirror. You can't imagine how much you look like I did when I was your age. What did you do to yourself?" Abigail's mother stood next to Mrs. Kindred.

"A cut-and-dye job," said Abigail sheepishly.

Her mother shook her head. "Honestly . . ." Then she noticed Timothy. "Who are you?"

"I'm Timothy," he answered, shoving his hands into his pockets. "Timothy July."

"We're working on a school project together," Abigail added.

Mrs. Kindred stepped forward and turned on the

hall light. She looked older than she had earlier in the week. Weary. She held on to the wall, as if to steady herself. "You're the boy from the museum," she said, squinting at him.

"Yes, ma'am," Timothy managed. Now he wasn't worried about her freaking out; instead, he worried she might murder him.

"How nice that you brought home a friend, Abigail," she said, softening. Timothy was unsure if she was just being polite. "I'm Zilpha." She glanced at Abigail's mother. "This is my daughter, Sarah."

"Nice to meet you," he whispered.

"Abigail, go clean up, then let's all sit down," said Sarah. "Gramma's had a long day." She took the old woman's hand and led her into the next room.

"I can manage, my dear," said Zilpha. "I'm not dead yet, you know."

"Can Timothy stay for supper?" Abigail asked.

"Fine with me," said Sarah. "Is it okay with your parents?"

"Uh . . . yeah," he answered, knowing that probably wasn't true.

Abigail and Timothy set the table as her grandmother sat at the far end of the dining room. When Abigail raised the question about what business her grandmother had at the museum the other day, Zilpha blushed and muttered something about inspiration, then quickly changed the subject to talk about the weather.

They were interrupted when Sarah brought a salad to the table. "Oh, Mom, I forgot to tell you, I finally met Georgia's new boyfriend." She turned to Timothy. "Georgia's our next-door neighbor. She and he were coming up in the elevator together earlier today. I admire her. At her age . . . It's never too late to start dating again, you know."

"Hmm. But where would *I* find the time, dear?" Zilpha smiled.

Sarah chuckled and turned toward the doorway. "Pasta's almost ready."

Silence filled the room. Timothy and Abigail glanced at each other. He waited for her to say something, but she nodded at him conspicuously. "So . . . uh, we're working on a book report," he said, blushing.

Abigail added, "A combination book report–history

project. That's why Mr. Crane brought our class to the museum."

"How nice," said Zilpha. "What book are you reading?"

"Oh, you've probably never heard of it," said Timothy, staring at his plate. "It's really old."

"In case you haven't noticed," said Zilpha, "I'm really old too."

They all laughed. Timothy quietly added, "It's called *The Clue of the Incomplete Corpse.*"

Overcome, the old woman went into a coughing fit for several seconds. After she recovered, she tentatively asked, "Where did you find a book with such a morbid title?"

Timothy glanced at Abigail. "By chance," Abigail answered for him. "It just sort of came to us."

"It *came* to you?"

"I've already read about half of it. We've started doing some research," said Timothy, trying to sound more assured. "The author was a lawyer from Boston. Strange." He thought carefully before adding, "I think his last name was the same as yours."

The old woman stared at the table now, her mouth set in a grimace. Finally, Zilpha said, "My uncle wrote several books when I was a girl, but under a pseudonym. Oswald Kent? Kentwall? Something like that. I don't really remember."

"That's it," said Abigail. "Ogden Kentwall."

"We learned his real last name online. But your last name is still . . . ?" Timothy was unsure how to finish.

"I kept 'Kindred' for professional reasons," she said. "I was a photographer in my youth."

"Abigail showed me the pictures," said Timothy. "They're amazing."

A spark lit up the old woman's eyes as she looked at him again. "Well . . . thank you."

"Gramma," said Abigail, "do you remember your uncle's books? They say he based the character on his niece." She quietly added, "Was it you?"

"I don't know what my uncle was thinking back then," said Zilpha. She hesitated before adding, "It's been a long time since *I've* thought about it."

"Can you tell us what happened?" asked Timothy.

"I . . . I don't remember much."

"Gramma, please. It'll really help . . . our report."

Zilpha shut her eyes, looking ready to close up entirely.

As one last desperate attempt for an answer, Timothy said, "Have you ever heard these names: Carlton Quigley, Bucky Jenkins, or Leroy Fromm?"

Now Zilpha looked truly confused. "Some stories are best forgotten," she said, shaking her head with finality. "Why don't you read something more fun, instead? I've heard so much about those Harry Potter books."

Abigail glanced at Timothy. The look in her eyes said, *This is not going to be easy.*

21.

After dinner, Timothy asked the location of the bus stop, so he could ride back up Edgehill Road to Beech Nut Street. Abigail's grandmother did not like that idea. "It's too late," she said. "Too dark."

As Sarah put on her coat, Abigail pulled Timothy into the living room. "We'll talk more tomorrow," she said.

"Right," said Timothy. "Tomorrow."

Outside, as Abigail's mother pulled her SUV away from the curb, Timothy noticed someone exiting the building.

A formidable silhouette heading north underneath the nearest streetlight. A tall man in a long overcoat. A small hat was perched on his head.

Timothy pressed his face to the window, craning his neck to keep the man in view as the SUV moved up the street. In the brief moment when Sarah paused to make a left onto Andrade Avenue, Timothy thought he saw the man pass into the shadows beyond the building. The sight sent shivers through him. He pressed himself into the passenger seat.

People often wore long coats and hats outside on cool nights. Was it possible that the sight of this man had meant nothing? He decided to call Abigail when he got home, just to be safe.

"Timothy! Where have you been?" his mother shouted at him when he came through the front door. The entire first floor of the house was lit up.

"I was at my friend Abigail's house," he said, slipping out of his wet sneakers and kicking them into the front hall closet.

"Why didn't you call?" said his mother, stepping into the doorway from the kitchen. "We were so worried. Your father was just about to notify the police. Plus, your school phoned that you had detention this afternoon. *What* is going on with you?"

"It was for passing a note in class," Timothy explained, shoving his hands deep in his pockets. "Mr. Crane was being totally unfair."

"That's not for you to decide," his father shouted from the kitchen. "Next time, you'd better call."

Something was going on here. Timothy could sense a change in the atmosphere; his parents were electrified. Last night, they hadn't cared that he'd walked home alone from the pool, but now . . .

"We got a call from your brother's doctor," said Timothy's mother. "They feel that he's been stabilized enough to transport him to a base in Maryland. He's on his way there right now."

Timothy grabbed on to the banister at the base of the stairs to steady himself. "Is he awake?"

"Not yet," she said. "But there's hope. I'm flying down first thing tomorrow."

"Can we all go?"

"They don't think that's a good idea, honey. Maybe eventually, but for now, I'm going alone to sort out the situation."

"What about Dad?"

"He'll stay here with you," said his mom. She held open her arms. Timothy came forward, and she hugged him. "You boys will take care of each other."

Timothy sat at the kitchen table and listened to his parents discuss their plans for the next few days. His mind was swirling with questions. "Have you heard anything about Stuart?"

His mother looked up from a pad of paper she'd been writing on. His father just looked confused.

"Stuart Chen," said Timothy. "Is he okay?"

"I'm sorry, honey," she said. "We've had too much on our minds. Why don't you try calling over there? Maybe he's home now."

Timothy stood up and went over to the phone hanging on the wall next to the refrigerator, but before he had a chance to pick it up, it rang. Surprised, he quickly answered it. "Hello?"

"You little monster." The voice was familiar, but Timothy was so shocked by the tone that it took him several seconds to place it.

"Mr. Crane?"

"Don't play all innocent with me, Mr. July," said Timothy's teacher. His voice shook, furious. "You know what you've done. And I do not appreciate it."

"Mr. Crane," Timothy said slowly, "I don't know what you're talking about."

"I'll give you a clue," said Mr. Crane. "The jars."

"The what?"

"The jars I requested you throw away after school this afternoon. Where, may I ask, did you throw them, exactly?"

"I took them outside and left them next to the garbage bin. The box was too heavy to lift," he answered.

"Why then, may I ask you, have they appeared on the front steps of my house?"

Timothy was so astounded he couldn't speak. The hum of the refrigerator killed the overwhelming silence. He glanced at his parents, who were now staring at him. His father mouthed, *Who is that?* Timothy turned away and stared at the floral wallpaper.

"I don't know why, Mr. Crane," said Timothy. "I didn't do it." The Nightmarys had told Abigail they'd helped her. Could this have been part of their game?

"Right. Just like you didn't throw the water balloon at the museum. Just like you didn't try to pass a note to Abigail Tremens during class today," said Mr. Crane. A few seconds later, he added, "Are your parents home?"

"They're right here," Timothy answered.

"I'd like to speak with one of them, please."

In a daze, Timothy held out the phone to his mother, stretching the long cord tight.

Timothy spent the rest of the night in his bedroom, both dreading and looking forward to the next day. He insisted to his parents that he hadn't pulled the prank on Mr. Crane, and thankfully, they believed him.

Just before he brushed his teeth, he remembered that he still hadn't called Abigail. He looked at the clock. It was nearly ten now. Much too late. He didn't want to bother anyone, especially Zilpha, who, according to Abigail's mother, needed her rest. Besides, the man he'd seen had probably been nobody.

When he turned off his light and got under his covers, Timothy imagined the specter of two girls watching him from the corner of his room. If what Abigail had told him was true, what sort of horror might they make next?

22.

Timothy woke up early the next morning when his mother knocked on his door to say goodbye. He wished he could go with her.

Later, Timothy was standing on the front porch, waiting for the bus, when he heard the Chens' screen door slam. Timothy rushed to the railing, leaned forward, and called to Stuart's mom, "How is he?"

She smiled a wan smile. "Technically, he's okay," she called back. "I think the whole thing has shaken him up a bit."

Timothy understood the feeling.

"He could use a friend," she added, making her way down the driveway toward her car. "Come by the hospital after school, if you can? They said he could have visitors. He'd love to see you."

"I'll try," said Timothy, even though he was frightened by what Stuart might have to say.

As Mrs. Chen pulled away from the curb, Timothy heard the phone ringing inside his house. Maybe it was his mom, calling from the airport? Since his dad had already gone to work, Timothy pulled out his keys, opened the door, and lifted the receiver.

"Hello?" he said.

The connection was bad. Static hissed as he waited for a response.

"Timothy?" The familiar voice on the other end was soft, ragged, as if it hadn't been used in a very long time. The room spun. Timothy reached out for the wall. He wondered if this wasn't some terrible trick. It had to be. There was no way he could possibly be on the phone with his brother.

"Yeah?"

"Oh my God, dude," said the voice. "Don't sound so excited to hear me."

"B-Ben?" Timothy stammered. "Is that you?"

"Sure, it's me." Ben laughed. But then the laugh turned into a cough, which went on for a long time. "Hold on . . . Water." A few seconds later, he added, "Sorry about that. Not been feeling too good lately."

Despite feeling baffled, Timothy smiled, but soon he felt tears coming. He didn't even bother fighting them. "Ben, are you okay? Where are you?"

“Some hospital. They tell me I’ve been asleep for a while?”

“You could say that,” said Timothy. “How long have you been awake?”

“In and out for the past twelve hours, I think. Everything’s a blur.”

“Mom’s flying down. She should be there soon.”

“That’s what my doctors told me. But I really wanted to

talk with someone I know . . . and love. My family. Dad must be on his way to work, but I thought I’d catch you before school. God, it’s so good to hear your voice.”

Questions flooded Timothy’s brain. Not only about the attack. He wanted to ask his big brother’s advice about finding order in chaos. The light in the darkness. Even though it sort of felt selfish, now might be his only chance for a while. *If you were in my situation . . .* “Are you in pain?” Timothy said instead.

Ben groaned. “They got me doped up pretty good. Attached to all sorts of tubes.”

“What do you remember?”

“Not much since before deployment. Weird. Most everything else is a big blank page. They say it’s going to take a long time to recover. Obviously an understatement. It’s like there’s a huge chunk of my life missing.”

Missing. The word made Timothy cringe. “I miss you,” he said.

“I was dreaming about you, little brother.”

"You were?"

Ben chuckled again. Or coughed. Timothy couldn't tell which. "It was a nightmare. Really scary."

"What was it about?"

"I was walking down a desert road," said Ben, struggling. "Sand everywhere. You were there. Strange thing was, you were holding a grenade and smiling in a really weird way. Your smile just kept growing and growing until your mouth was bigger than your face."

A horrible image. Timothy blinked it away. "That *is* weird," he said.

Ben went on. "Then you held the grenade out to me. You wanted me to take it. And right before I did, I realized that you'd already pulled the pin." Timothy felt his face flush. He felt dizzy now. Then, with his voice crackling, Ben added, "It's your fault this happened to me. It's your fault I'm dead."

Timothy tried to speak but couldn't.

Silence hissed from the other end of the line; then Ben began to laugh. The laughter turned harsh, sinking into a deep pitch as it grew louder and louder. It was no longer Ben's voice. And it was no longer only in the phone. The laughter surrounded him, bouncing off the walls of the foyer, filling the entire house. Timothy crouched into a ball and covered his head to try to block it out.

Suddenly, a siren screamed. He fell against the wooden bench. Timothy looked at the receiver in his hand. A busy signal blared at him through the holes in the plastic. Then a tinny female voice shouted, "If you'd like to make a call, please hang up and try again. If you need help, please dial—"

A door slammed. Timothy dropped the phone and glanced upstairs. "H-hello?" he called. No one answered. Dizzy with fear, Timothy stood, replaced the phone on the cradle, and listened to the house's overwhelming silence.

Outside, an engine sputtered. His bus was turning up Beech Nut Street. Timothy opened the front door and ran to catch it.

23.

A stranger sat behind Mr. Crane's desk—a substitute. Mr. Crane was out sick.

Timothy snuck to his seat in the back of the classroom. The rest of the students slowly began to trickle in. Moments later, when the class was nearly full, a new girl with short black hair appeared in the doorway. No one seemed to notice her. She gave him the smallest, most hidden smile he'd ever witnessed. It was their secret now, one of many.

The bell rang, and the substitute teacher stood up and read from a piece of paper. "Please move to be with your partner, and work on your project."

Timothy got up and sat down in the desk next to Abigail. "What's wrong?" she said. "You look a little odd."

"I wonder where Mr. Crane is." He was still trying to

recover from his frightful phone call. He kept remembering the sound of his brother's laughter.

"After you left last night," she said, shaking her head, "all hell broke loose at my house."

"What do you mean?"

"My grandmother got really upset that we had been asking her about that book her uncle wrote. She said she doesn't want me to hang out with you anymore."

Timothy's face burned. "She doesn't like me?"

"It's not that. I think she's trying to protect us from something."

"From what?"

"She didn't tell me."

"If we knew the truth," he said, "we would know what we're up against."

"To be fair, we didn't tell her the truth either."

"Yeah, but . . ." Timothy thought about that. It would be impossible to explain the events of this week to anyone who hadn't experienced them too. "But should we? Your grandmother is obviously keeping a secret. Maybe we should tell her ours."

"I don't know if that's a good idea. If she wasn't so weird about the whole thing . . ." Abigail stared at her desk. "I slept on the couch in the living room, if sleeping is what you want to call it. I waited all night for those girls to show up. They didn't, thank God. Maybe my disguise worked."

"I almost forgot! You'll never believe what else I saw . . . or maybe you will at this point, actually." Timothy finally told her about the man he'd seen leaving her apartment building.

Abigail nearly fell out of her chair. "Why didn't you call me?"

Timothy explained what had happened when he'd gotten home—about Ben's transport to Maryland and Mr. Crane's call. "I sort of forgot about everything else," he added. "Sorry." Finally, he told her about Ben's phone call that morning.

"Are you sure it was him?" said Abigail, the color draining from her face.

"It sounded like him. Maybe someone's trying to screw with us?"

"But who?" she said.

Timothy was about to suggest that the call might have been from Abigail's Nightmarys, but she continued, "And who was the guy you saw at my building? Was *he* real? Do you think it was your shadow man?"

"Could've been anybody, I guess. Have you seen anyone like that there before?"

Abigail shook her head. "No. But I haven't really been looking." After a moment, she said, "Hey, did you check the jars yet?" When Timothy gave her a blank look, she continued, "Didn't Mr. Crane say you left them on his front steps? I wonder if the box you put in the parking lot is still there."

"Doesn't matter," said Timothy. "Don't they empty the Dumpsters every night?"

Abigail sighed. "I can't help remembering what the Nightmarys said to me. That they had 'helped' me, and now I *have* to go with them. Are they still 'helping' me? You're seeing and hearing creepy stuff. Mr. Crane is obviously bugging out. Stuart's in the hospital. If that is all part of this, then the Nightmarys must think I owe them. Maybe if I go with them, all the rest will stop."

"No freakin' way!" Timothy shouted. "Don't even think that."

Abigail blushed. "But where do they want to take me? And why?" She stared at the floor. "What if they find me? What if I can't say no the next time they ask me to go?"

"You always have a choice," said Timothy, unsure if it was the right thing to say.

Abigail seemed to shudder, then said, "I've got an idea." The bell rang, marking the end of class. "Remember that Web site you said you found with my great-great-uncle's author biography?"

"Ogden Kentwall?"

"Right. Well, I was thinking, since my grandmother probably won't tell us her story, maybe we should write to the Web site. Try to get some more information."

Timothy nodded, excited. "Yeah. Like, how does the book end?"

"Exactly. Maybe there is an *actual* clue to an incomplete corpse."

Together, they walked to the library and opened the Web site. "We'll just ask her if she can provide us with any more information about the book's history," said Abigail. "Maybe even a plot summary . . . I hope this woman, the owner, won't think we're cheating on a class project."

Timothy shrugged. "At this point a little cheating is in order. If she asks, we'll tell her someone stole our only copy."

"Hey," said Abigail, "at least it won't be a lie."

Waiting for the end of the day, Timothy floated through the rest of his classes. Then he met Abigail, and Abigail logged into her e-mail account. To their amazement, there was a response from the owner of the bookstore.

From: frances@
To: lilbadwolf97@
Subject: The Clue of the Incomplete Corpse

Dear Abigail,

Thank you for your inquiry. I am always happy to oblige a literature lover's rare-book pursuit. I understand your financial and time constraints, so I am absolutely willing to help answer your questions, the first obviously concerning the plot of

Ogden Kentwall's debut mystery novel for children. As you've stated, you understand the basic premise of the book–Zelda Kite, girl reporter, searches for her missing classmate. Fairly standard mid-twentieth-century stuff. But about halfway through the novel, the story takes quite a dark turn. The darkness stems from a magical object Zelda learns of, which supposedly gives its user the power to control other people's fear. In this case, I think the object was the jawbone of some sort of ancient goddess. I don't remember how it worked, except that whoever wielded it simply targeted the person they meant to frighten, and then made a wish. The jawbone's magic would penetrate the victim's mind, driving him mad in the process.

The plot of this book pales in comparison to some of the creepy things children read nowadays, but as I said in my online description, the book does have its charms. Zelda Kite is a strong, quirky female character, with oodles of savvy and wit. I do hate to spoil the ending of the book for you, but since you asked, I'll go ahead with it. If you wish to be surprised, you may want to stop here.

By closely examining a photograph she took at the Fourth of July Parade, Zelda Kite realizes she'd captured the moment of her friend's abduction. She uses this evidence to track down a professor at the local college. Eventually she learns that this is the man who has taken her friend, with the dubious purpose of using the girl to somehow charge this magical jawbone. You see, the bone maintains its power through a sacrifice to the ancient goddess. This professor has been keeping the poor girl locked in a hidden room at the college where he works until the time is right to make the sacrifice and charge the bone. Lots more mumbo jumbo ensues, but the point is, Zelda Kite rescues her friend and becomes a local hero.

I actually sought out *The Clue of the Incomplete Corpse* after I learned of its strange origin at a booksellers' convention several years ago. Supposedly, in the 1940s, Mr. Kentwall's niece was a reporter, or maybe a photographer, for her school newspaper. One of her classmates was in fact abducted by a prominent local man, a professor at New Starkham College, in Massachusetts. Mr. Kentwall's added mysticism aside, I'm not entirely sure of the real story, but I believe that Kentwall's niece was not pleased to have been turned into a literary celebrity. I imagine the real experience was quite harrowing for her, especially since in reality her own friend was never found.

I'm not sure how much more I can help you, other than with the small bits of information I've already provided. There do not appear to be any New Starkham newspaper archives online from that time just yet. But if you are curious and able to make a visit to New Starkham, I'm sure one of the local libraries would be able to help track down an article or two to flesh out additional details.

I hope I was able to provide some worthy assistance. Please let me know if you may be eventually interested in a copy of the book. My own son and his friends have enjoyed reading the series very much, and I believe you may too.

Yours truly,
Frances May
Owner and Proprietress—
The Enigmatic Manuscript Bookstore
Gatesweed, Massachusetts

"Hmm," said Timothy. "Do you think we'll have time to make a visit to the library in New Starkham? It's so far away."

At that, Abigail laughed, hard.

24.

Timothy and Abigail decided to go to the hospital after their trip to the town library that afternoon. He knew it would be weird to arrive with Abigail but felt it was really important that they both hear Stuart describe what he'd experienced at the pool. At the very least, they would see how he was doing, even if Stuart didn't expect or even want to see Abigail.

When they arrived at the library, to their extreme disappointment, they found the microfiche unavailable. The librarian explained that all their film and fiche were being digitized, but they should try back next week. Discouraged, they left and walked toward Howard Square, where, several blocks ahead, the ten-story tower of New Starkham Hospital rose like a white marble monument.

* * *

In the elevator, Timothy felt claustrophobic. The car brought them swiftly upward.

"Timothy!" cried Mrs. Chen softly when they reached the room. Standing in the hall, she grabbed him and squeezed tight. "You came. I'm so glad."

"Yeah, I skipped swim practice tonight."

Mrs. Chen looked at Abigail and struggled to hold on to her spontaneous smile.

"This is . . . Abigail," said Timothy. "She wanted to see Stuart too."

"*Abigail?*" said Mrs. Chen. She'd obviously heard the name before. That smile became more of a struggle. "It's . . . nice to meet you. Please, come in."

Stuart was sitting in his bed, hugging his knees, staring at the blanket. A large snapdragon bouquet sat on the side table. Mrs. Chen made her way to the table, conspicuously silent, and began to fiddle with the arrangement. Timothy paused in the doorway. When Stuart saw Timothy, he burst into tears. "I'm so sorry. I'm so sorry. You were right! I was such a fart-slap." Mrs. Chen flinched, pretending not to hear that.

Timothy froze. Abigail was hidden several steps behind him.

"You don't have to apologize," said Timothy.

"Yes, I do. You don't understand. She's going to come back if I don't. And I don't want to think about what she'll bring next time."

Mrs. Chen rested her palm on his forehead. She looked nervously toward the door, as if contemplating calling the nurse. "Now, Stuart. Timothy came to see you. Calm down. Okay?"

"Who . . . ," Timothy began, "who's going to come back?"

Mrs. Chen threw him a look, as if to say, *Please don't start.* But Timothy couldn't help it. He needed to know.

"The girl."

"What girl?"

Tears were streaming down Stuart's face now. "Please. You have to forgive me. That's the only way to make it stop."

Mrs. Chen came toward Timothy and pulled him away from the bed. She whispered, "He's been having these delusions since they brought him here. They're running tests to see what might be causing them."

"They're not delusions," said Stuart, from his bed.

"Can we . . . ," Timothy began, "can *I* have a second alone with Stuart? I think I might be able to help."

Mrs. Chen glanced at Abigail, who was standing in the hallway, still outside Stuart's field of vision. Abigail held her hands in front of herself. She looked terrified. "I suppose a short time alone will be all right," said Stuart's mother hesitantly. "But if he starts throwing things at . . . the corner of the room, please call me immediately."

"The corner of the room?" said Timothy.

Mrs. Chen shook her head, then left and closed the door

behind her. Once the latch clicked, Stuart leaned forward again. "You came," he said. "That has to mean something." His pupils were large, as if he was sitting in a room much darker than this one.

"Yeah," said Timothy. "Well, I wanted to make sure you're okay. I saw Coach Thom pull you out of the water."

"You're here," said Stuart, ignoring what Timothy was saying. "Everything's going to go back to the way it was before, now. Right?"

"Before?" said Timothy, sitting on the end of the bed. "Before what?"

"Before *she* came," Stuart whispered.

"Who?"

"Abigail." He said her name so harshly Timothy felt a hole open in his stomach. What would Stuart do when he found out *she* was standing in the hallway?

Still, Timothy answered, "Everything's exactly the same as it used to be." It felt weird lying to Stuart, but Stuart looked like he needed to be lied to. "I'm here. It's all good. Everything is going to be fine now." Stuart smiled a true smile. "Hey, I have a favor to ask."

Stuart leaned away, cautious. "What is it?"

"Tell me what you've being seeing."

"What do you mean?"

"Tell me about . . . your monster."

* * *

Timothy was surprised at how easily Stuart opened up. Randy Weiss's story had been right. Stuart believed he'd seen the *Wraith Wars* claw monster at the bottom of the pool, that it had dragged him under.

The first night in the hospital, he began to hear a voice from underneath his bed. It told him that his "accident" had happened because of what he'd done at the museum. Abigail was angry at him now—a bad thing. The next morning, after he told a nurse about the voice, the doctors became even more concerned.

"They think I'm crazy," said Stuart, "but I know I'm not."

Timothy nodded. "I know you're not either."

"*How* do you know that?"

"Because I've known you forever," said Timothy, with finality. "I mean, I've always thought you were a little weird, but crazy? Come on."

Stuart smiled weakly. Then he continued his story.

The night before, Stuart lay awake, expecting the voice to return. Sometime after midnight, he heard a noise at the foot of his bed. He sat up and whispered, "Who's there?" Slowly, a tall, skinny girl rose up and clutched the bed frame. Stuart was too frightened to even scream. In the darkness, he couldn't make out her face, but somehow he knew she was Abigail—a nightmare version even though he was awake.

"Sorry yet?" Abigail had asked.

"Yes!" Stuart had answered. "Yes, I'm very sorry. Please, leave me alone."

"I don't believe you. You don't mean it."

"I do mean it! I've never been sorrier."

She laughed. "I'll know when you're *really* sorry," Abigail said. She glanced at the darkest corner of the room, beside the drawn window curtain. "He'll tell."

"Who?" said Stuart. "Who will tell?" The girl was gone, but Stuart knew he was not alone. He strained to see beyond the shadows into the far corner of the room, where the girl had glanced before disappearing. His eyes adjusted to the darkness. He finally made out a figure dressed in a shapeless black robe, propped rigidly against the wall. Small, shiny black eyes stared out from a pale, hairless, and doughy face. Terrified, Stuart grabbed the glass of water off the nightstand and flung it into the corner of the room. It shattered above the figure's head, but the thing did not move or even respond. It only continued to watch him.

Then the nurses came. They turned on the lights. The corner was now empty. Stuart screamed and struggled and fought, until the nurses gave him a sedative that made him feel sleepy and weak. He begged them to keep the lights on, to stay with him awhile longer, and they did. But later, even in his dreams, the thing in the corner of the room watched him, waiting until he was *really* sorry for what he had done.

No one believed his story. In fact, the more he insisted on its truth, the more they wanted to keep him there for observation.

Timothy sat at the end of the bed, stunned. Stuart had seen an Abigail, the same way Abigail said she had seen the Nightmarys.

Stuart glanced past Timothy and cringed. Timothy turned. "Hi, Stuart," said Abigail. She stood just inside the room, looking embarrassed. "Timothy and I came to see how you're doing."

"Mom!" Stuart called.

"She's talking with a nurse down the hall," said Abigail quietly. "She'll be back soon."

"Please," said Stuart. "Just take that thing out of here."

Anger flashed in Abigail's eyes. "What did you just call me?"

"Not you," Stuart pleaded. "The thing. The *thing* you put in the corner of the room."

Abigail glanced at Timothy. She raised her eyebrow. "I've never been in this room until me and Timothy came tonight. I promise." He now understood she'd overheard Stuart's story. They both looked at the corner of the room near the window. To them, it was empty.

"Is he staring at you right now?" Timothy asked. Stuart

pursed his lips and nodded discreetly. "Why don't you just ask him to leave?"

"He'll get mad. I know it."

"But there's nothing there," said Abigail.

Silence fell. The three of them stared at each other for a while before Timothy could think to say, "We've *all* been seeing scary things this week, Stuart. Not just you."

"You have?"

Abigail nodded, then glanced to the corner of the room. "Yes. We have."

"We, who?" said Stuart.

"Me and Abigail," said Timothy. "And Mr. Crane."

"Mr. Crane?" said Stuart. "Why? What kind of scary things?"

Timothy thought of a simple explanation. "A man has been following me. And Abigail has been seeing . . . ghosts. And Mr. Crane—"

"So *you're* not making these things happen to me?" Stuart asked Abigail.

She looked guilty but shook her head and said, "I wouldn't even know where to begin to learn something like that."

"Then how?" said Stuart. "Why?"

"That's what we're trying to figure out," said Timothy.

"We want to help you," Abigail added, almost reluctantly.

"Help me? Why would *you* want to help me?"

"Because you obviously need it."

Stuart finally appeared to get it. Folding his hands in his lap, he quietly said, "If you want to help me, please, just accept my apology."

Abigail came forward out of the doorway and grabbed on to the end of Stuart's bed. "It was just a stupid water balloon," she said. "I've already forgotten all about it."

Red-eyed, Stuart licked his lips and glanced into the corner of the room. "Then why is he still standing there?" he asked in a very small, very frightened voice. "Why is he still staring at me?"

25.

"What's wrong?" said Abigail. They were standing at the bus stop, just outside the hospital entrance. The wind had picked up. Thunder rolled across the river. "You haven't said a word since we said goodbye to Stuart's mother." She was right, but Timothy was too busy feeling overwhelmed to notice.

He suddenly felt a surge of indescribable anger. "Hmm, let's see. What's wrong?" he echoed Abigail. "Oh, I don't know. Maybe it's that I just realized my best friend has lost his mind, and I'm beginning to feel pretty much the same way." Timothy wiped his nose. "My brother's in a coma. My parents won't talk to me. And—"

"Hey," Abigail said softly, "you don't have to snap at me. I'm just asking a question."

"I'm not snapping," Timothy continued, knowing that was exactly what he'd been doing. "I'm just . . . I'm just . . ." He finally looked at her. She was squinting at him, trying to figure him out, like she always seemed to be doing whenever he caught her looking at him. "I'm sorry."

They heard an engine shift gears as two bright headlights came around the far corner of the building. Through the wet window, the bus driver looked unhappy to stop. The rest of the bus was empty. They stepped inside and paid

the fare.

Sitting together, Abigail looked at Timothy's reflection in the window. They were transparent, like ghosts. "I still don't get it," she said. "We don't know anything more than we did before."

"But that's not true."

"Okay," said Abigail, nodding. "What do we know?"

"We know that Stuart blames you for what happened to him." Timothy watched as Abigail soaked in that information. She looked like she wasn't sure how to feel about it. "We know that he saw almost exactly what you saw."

"Which would be?"

"A girl," said Timothy. "But *he* thought she was you, not some brats from New Jersey."

Abigail drew away from him, as if she couldn't believe what she was hearing. "So what . . . he's scared of me?"

"You could've told the thing in the corner to go away."

"There was nothing there!"

"It would've helped! Stuart was terrified of it." Timothy

felt an odd tightening in his chest. He kept thinking back to the conversation he'd had that morning with his brother, or the *thing* that was pretending to be his brother. "According to the message from the owner of that bookstore, *The Clue of the Incomplete Corpse* is based on true events. She wrote that in the book there was some sort of object, a bone that gives you the power to control other people's fears. Right?"

"It's just a stupid book, Timothy." Now Abigail started to look nervous, as if Timothy was talking crazy.

"But part of it *happened*, or at least we're pretty sure it did." Abigail blinked and shook her head. Timothy continued, "*Someone* is screwing with what makes us afraid. Stuart's claw monster. Mr. Crane and the things in those jars. That phone call and my brother's injury. I mean, I've been having nightmares about Ben for a while, but only when I'm asleep. *This* is totally different." Abigail sighed and started to speak, but he cut her off. "Let me finish. I know you said you never wanted to hurt anyone—"

"Timothy!"

"I know you said that, but Stuart obviously made you angry, and you certainly got mad at Mr. Crane in the museum. And me . . ." Timothy took a deep breath. "You said it yourself that first day I asked to be your partner. You thought I was picking on you. You wanted me to stay away from you."

"So what?" Now Abigail was fuming.

"So? There you have it. Three reasons to want to get back

at the three people, besides you, *supposedly*, who've all of a sudden started seeing some really creepy stuff."

"We already went over all this," said Abigail. "Last night when you came over, I told you that the Nightmarys are doing it. They wanted to help me. I never asked them to! They want me to follow them—"

"Right. The Nightmarys. Who just happened to show up at your apartment because they wanted to be your friend. And play games. In the middle of the night."

"You don't believe me?"

"I believed you before I found out about this *jawbone thing*," said Timothy, the words pouring from him. "What if someone found it and learned how to use it?"

"You think it's me?" said Abigail.

Timothy's skin tingled as he remembered. "The museum."

"What about it?"

"Remember, just before we found *The Edge of Doom*? We saw that poster that talked about magic and religion? There was an artifact in the case that was supposed to give one tribe the power to control their victim's fear. The instructions were printed right there. Hold the thing. Name the victim. Place a curse."

"A jawbone," Abigail whispered, turning pale. "But someone had removed it for cleaning."

"Your grandmother was there that day, she said for inspiration, but what the heck does *that* mean?"

Abigail's mouth dropped open. A few seconds later, she managed to say, "Don't tell me you think Gramma—"

"I have no idea what to think," Timothy interrupted. The windows were totally fogged with their breath, their reflections gone. They could only stare at each other now.

"Well, you want to know what I think?" Abigail shouted. She didn't wait for an answer. She stuck out her finger and wrote on the window, carving into the fog in enormous block letters: U-SUCK. Then she pressed the yellow plastic strip that ran vertically up the wall next to the window, ringing the bell for the bus to stop.

A few seconds later, the driver pulled up to the curb and opened the door.

"What are you doing?" Timothy asked.

"I'm walking," said Abigail, flinging herself out of her seat.

"Yeah, but where are you going?" he called.

She practically ran to the front door. "To *disappear.*" Timothy scrambled to catch up. Just before she stepped out onto the wet curb, she turned and said, "It's just a stupid book." She shook her head, disappointed. "There's *no such thing* as a magical jawbone, Timothy. That's the dumbest thing I've ever heard. You . . . *butt-munch.*" She started walking up the street, away from the bus.

Timothy didn't know what to do. He couldn't just let her stomp home alone in the dark, not after everything that had happened, not after knowing all the things that might be out there waiting for her. But then he realized that he *had* just sort of blamed her for orchestrating the whole thing, which, if true, would make her safe after all.

Stupid stupid stupid! he wanted to scream.

"On or off?" said the driver, rolling his eyes.

"I'm off!" shouted Timothy, leaping onto the curb. The door closed swiftly, and before he could even think, the bus was pulling away into the night, its brake lights blurring red through the mist.

Timothy called out, "Abigail!" He listened for a moment, to see if he could hear her. From the river, the old foghorn wailed. The thunder called again, its voice a low growl. A streetlamp threw a hazy glow across the darkened storefront windows ahead. Timothy thought he could make out the shape of a girl running away from him, her silhouette becoming fainter and fainter as the shadows swallowed her up.

26.

After running half a block, Timothy had lost sight of her. Other than the sound of the growing wind and the continuous rumble of thunder in the distance, the street was quiet. He'd been thinking aloud on the bus, but he hadn't meant to hurt Abigail's feelings. He needed to apologize. Maybe he'd find her at the Mayfair? Timothy turned up his collar and began the ascent up the hill. What if she wouldn't forgive him?

Several blocks ahead, Timothy froze. A dark figure appeared before him, standing underneath a streetlight. At first, Timothy thought it might be the shadow man. Then he realized that this figure was not nearly as tall. He also wasn't wearing that long overcoat. No, this new figure wore a different kind of outfit. A tight-fitting uniform. As Timothy took another step forward, he noticed that the figure leaned against a crutch. "Ben?" he whispered.

Then the figure turned around and began to walk away.

Remembering the horrible conversation from that morning, Timothy hesitated, but as the figure continued up the hill, he again called out, "Ben!" By the time he reached the next stop sign, the figure was only half a block ahead. When Timothy called out one more time, the figure only continued his silent journey, as if he couldn't hear his little brother, or

didn't care to respond. The rain began to fall harder now, blurring the night. Timothy wiped at his eyes, but the next time he looked up the street, the figure had disappeared.

Before he knew it, Timothy was standing just down the block from his house. Where had the figure gone? Timothy struggled to breathe, just like after a fast sprint during swim practice. He was too far away from the Mayfair to walk there now. And he certainly didn't want to be alone. Shivering and afraid, he turned at the corner of Beech Nut, grateful that his house was just up the street.

Suddenly, the figure stepped out from behind a tall evergreen bush, and Timothy nearly tripped over his own feet. Ben grabbed at him, but he swerved out of his grasp.

Now they were face to face, and Timothy suddenly wished they weren't. Ben didn't look like Ben. His eyes were milky, his skin blotchy red. In fact, he looked a lot like Timothy's nightmare that week. Ben opened his mouth, revealing his brown rotting teeth. "This is your fault, Timothy," he said, his voice gritty. "You shouldn't have let me leave New Starkham. You should have told me to stay. . . ."

"What are you . . . ?" Timothy began, his voice shaking with disbelief. Were they really *talking* about this? As bizarre as the whole thing seemed, he couldn't stop himself from answering. "I shouldn't have let you leave? What about what you told me? You needed to find some order in all this chaos. What about your light in the darkness?"

Ben blinked, as if he hadn't heard. "This is your fault, Timothy. Your fault . . . But I forgive you." Ben smiled a horrible smile. He held his arms open. The crutch clattered to the sidewalk. "Here, give your brother a hug."

"You're not my brother!" said Timothy, pushing at the figure. But when his hands slipped through the figure into nothingness, Timothy realized he was standing alone in the street. Lightning flashed and almost immediately the thunder clapped. Ben was gone.

Timothy closed his eyes for several seconds, too frightened to move.

He didn't notice the headlights speeding toward him from the opposite direction.

27.

Timothy spun.

The lights blinded him as the car screeched to a stop. When he finally felt his heart restart, the car's horn nearly knocked him over again. He quickly stepped out of the way, back onto the safety of the curb, ready to raise a particular finger to whomever was driving this hunk of junk. Over the din of the rain hitting the car's hood, he heard the grinding gear of one of the windows rolling down.

"What the hell are you doing in the middle of the street?" The sound of his father's voice was nearly as shocking as the car horn moments earlier. "You looking to hitch a ride on the roadkill wagon?" Timothy's father sounded more worried than angry. Timothy felt so traumatized he couldn't even answer. "You're all wet. Get in." Timothy opened the door and slipped inside.

They sat quietly for a few seconds, listening to the rain drumming against the roof.

"So are you going to tell me what you were doing out there? Or are you going to make me guess?" said Timothy's father.

How could he tell his father about seeing zombie Ben, especially since Ben had simply disappeared? At best, his father would ignore him. At worst . . .

"I just walked home. Me and Abigail went to visit Stuart in the hospital."

"You should've called me for a ride. Who's Abigail?"

"A girl I go to school with."

"Hmm," said Timothy's father, his mind elsewhere. "I need you to do me a favor." He reached into the glove compartment, grabbed a set of keys, and handed them to Timothy. "Pull your mother's car into the garage. Keep to the right. I need to park this thing next to it."

Timothy felt a small rush. His father had never asked him to do this by himself before. It should have been more exciting. "Whose car is this?" Timothy asked, trying to sound peppy.

"I'm doing a favor for a buddy. Said I'd give it a look over the weekend." His father clicked the garage-door opener. Timothy hopped out of the car, clutching the keys. He'd watched his father do this plenty of times. He'd waited years for this chance. Now his mind was so frantic, he couldn't even think about enjoying the experience.

Once his father had pulled into the garage beside him, Timothy followed him out into the rain. "Nice job there," said his father, distracted. "Stuart's doing better?" His father led the way up the brick path toward the house's unlit back door.

"That's the big question," Timothy said, trailing behind. Lightning flashed again, and the memory of Ben's face echoed

in Timothy's mind. Suddenly, he remembered there were bigger questions.

THE

NIGHTMARYS

INTERLUDE

Marcella's Italian Restaurant—
Providence, Rhode Island

"Surprise!" shouted the crowd.

Percival Ankh clutched at his chest and screwed up his face into a mad grimace. Everyone gasped, but when Percival smiled, his family understood he was just kidding. Cruel, he knew, but he'd told them for years that he hated surprises. They deserved it. "Oh, Dad," they said, patting him on the back, wishing him congratulations.

The old man's family was throwing him a birthday party. He was ninety today, a late-April baby, a typically stubborn Taurus. He'd told his wife he'd never been sure he'd actually wanted to live this long. But now, surrounded by his loved ones, Percival realized what his life had been all about. Sure, there had always been the challenges of working at the library, but finding his family at home at the end of the day provided his true satisfaction.

The food was delicious, and the cake was even better.

Later, when Percival got up to use the restroom, everyone looked nervous. "I do this every day at home by myself," he said. "I can walk." Still, his son insisted on accompanying him. Percival waved him away. "How about this instead? If I'm not back in ten minutes, send out a search party."

After he'd done his business, Percival washed his hands. When he'd first entered the bathroom, an attendant had greeted him, smiling. Now, though, Percival was alone. Strange. He grabbed a towel to dry himself, then turned to go.

But the door he'd entered through was no longer there. Somehow, it had been replaced with a solid wall, covered by the dull, gray-striped wallpaper that encompassed the rest of the room, like bars. "What the . . . ?" said Percival, searching the room for a way out. He must have gotten turned around. But as he scanned each wall it seemed as though there actually was no exit.

He was trapped in here. Alone. Impossible. Was this another surprise, another trick planned by his kids to teach him a lesson for messing around earlier?

The old man pounded on the wall where the door should have been. He called out for his son. Boy, his kids were thinking, will Dad be embarrassed when he comes back to the table. Can't even pee by himself anymore, they'd say. Poor old guy.

He waited, but received no answer.

Then, behind him, one of the stall doors creaked open. Percival turned, chills swarming his body like little red ants. Maybe the attendant he'd seen earlier had been in there the whole time. Maybe he could help.

A man stepped out from the stall, but it was not the attendant. This man's face was familiar, though Percival hadn't thought of him in years . . . especially since the man he was staring at was dead. Percival fell backward against the wall.

The man in the gray overcoat pulled the small wicker basket from the counter between the sinks and held it out. Smiling, he said, "Soap? Lotion? Mint?" Then he began to laugh. Percival turned and pounded harder than ever on the wall behind him.

Where the hell was that search party?

28.

On Saturday morning, Timothy awoke with the sun shining in his eyes. Everything was, and always had been, fine.

Moments later, after a good stretch, Timothy sat up in his bed and realized that everything was not fine. The week's events came rushing back to him, and despite the revelatory light of the morning, he felt an awful dread, which grew when he heard the phone ringing.

Rushing downstairs, Timothy grabbed the handset from the side table in the front hallway. "Hello?"

"Timothy," said an old woman's voice. "This is Zilpha Kindred. Abigail's grandmother. Sorry to call so early, but I need your help."

Zilpha explained that the night before, Abigail had arrived home quite late, drenched from the rain. She'd apologized and asked if she could go to sleep early. Later, in bed, Zilpha was restless, so she went to get a glass of water. When she heard a sniffling noise outside the foyer, Zilpha opened the front door and found Abigail slumped against the wall. The elevator button glowed red. Zilpha led her back into the apartment. She asked Abigail what was going on. Breaking down, Abigail had told her everything.

"Everything?" Timothy asked.

"Everything," Zilpha answered. "And there are a few things you should know too, Timothy."

The night before, Zilpha had explained to Abigail that these odd occurrences were something they shared—that when Zilpha was young, she tried to stop a bad man from doing a bad thing. His name had been Christian Hesselius—the man Frances May had told them about. Now, somehow the bad man had returned to New Starkham to fulfill some kind of vengeance. The weirdest part? The bad man had died in an institution nearly fifty years ago.

"But how . . . ?" Timothy imagined his shadow man as a ghost, a magician, a demon.

"I'm not exactly sure myself," said Zilpha.

"Is Abigail okay now?"

"That's why I'm calling, Timothy. Did she say anything about leaving New Starkham to go back to her father in New Jersey?"

"Yes, actually," he answered quietly. "She told me she was thinking about it, but then changed her mind."

"She left a letter on the dining room table this morning.

She must have snuck out quite early." Timothy felt his throat begin to close. "We can't reach her father. Sarah has already left town to search for her. If you hear anything . . ."

"Uh-huh," Timothy murmured, his mind racing with guilt for not following Abigail all the way home.

"I beg you to call." Zilpha gave him her phone number, which he scribbled on a nearby scrap of paper. "And Timothy . . . trust me. After today, this will be over. I know everything must seem weird, but please . . . This is my mess, and I am handling it. Alone. Understand?"

"Okay," he said. Even though Timothy now had a million more questions, he still managed to hang up.

When he had finally collected his thoughts, Timothy poured himself a bowl of cereal, ate quickly, then packed his swim bag, sticking Zilpha's phone number in his pocket. If Zilpha didn't want him thinking about Christian Hesselius, he had to do something else. Saturday-morning practice would be starting in less than a half hour. He left a note on the counter, telling his father where he had gone.

The air outside was brisk, but not cold. As Timothy made his way down the hill toward Edgehill Road and the mouth of the Dragon Stairs, he hoped he could stop worrying about what might be waiting for him in the locker room.

* * *

Luckily, when he arrived, several of his team members were still in the dim chamber, putting on their suits, and teasing each other with the threat of rat-tail whips. Timothy changed, then followed the rowdy group through the showers and down the long hallway to the pool.

Timothy tried to follow Thom's practice to the minute. Whenever he swam toward the deep end, he couldn't help imagining what Stuart had seen at the bottom of the pool.
Under the diving platforms, he kept his eyes closed, and counted his strokes so he could find the wall.

"Nice work," Thom called out to him, after the first one hundred yards. "I've never seen you swim so fast." Timothy knew why: he'd never before felt like something was chasing him.

The more he thought about Zilpha's call, the more anxious he became. Maybe if he walked to the Mayfair now, they could talk some more, sort this out together. She was an old woman. Abigail would have wanted him to help her grandmother, wouldn't she?

From the shallow end, Timothy pushed off the wall, heading into a particularly strong free-style sprint. He had to beat the clock.

Head to Zilpha's apartment, even though she'd asked him to stay out of it. That's what he'd do. The route would be easy, up the southern slope, right past the college library—

Timothy felt a jolt, then jerked his body upright. Grabbing on to the closest lane line in the middle of the pool, he fought to keep from going under. The person swimming behind him just missed smacking him in the face with a butterfly upstroke. Timothy didn't even notice.

The library.

The college had a library too.

Maybe they would have the answers he needed?

This way, Zilpha wouldn't have to know.

29.

Outside, Timothy walked through the quad. He followed the stone path as it wound between the centuries-old buildings.

The hill rose as Timothy headed south, and suddenly he was standing in front of a tall structure that reminded him of the mansion from *The Addams Family.* Timothy pulled hard on the handle and slipped inside.

His eyes adjusted slowly to the difference in light. Two wings of the building reached out from a central distribution desk that sat directly in front of the main entrance. A blond girl with large blue eyes stood behind the desk.

"Hey, cutie," she said. "What can I do for ya?"

"I—I was wondering if I'm allowed to use the library," he stammered, blushing. "I've got to research a school project."

The girl laughed. "I'm assuming you don't have a college ID card."

Timothy shook his head.

"Are you here with that other girl?"

"What other girl?"

"Guess not," said the blond girl. "We don't usually have non–college students trying to get into the library on a daily basis. Two in one morning is just strange. You're lucky I'm not a stickler for the rules. If Gavin was around—"

"There's a girl here?" Timothy felt his heart start to pound. "My age?"

She nodded. "Here's a temporary card. If you need anything, just let me know." She slipped him a small piece of paper.

"Actually, I'm wondering if you have old copies of New Starkham newspapers. Like, from the 1940s?"

The girl stared at him for a moment, then said, "Okay, that's weird. The other girl asked me the same thing when she came in an hour ago. I already gave her all that microfiche. You're going to have to share." She pointed into the wing on Timothy's right. "The room is behind the last row of books. Careful. It's dark back there."

"Thanks," said Timothy, heading in the direction the girl had pointed. As he approached the last row of shelves, he knew who he'd find there.

* * *

"What are you doing here?" said Abigail when she saw him.

The faint backlight from the microfiche screen threw her face into shadow. Behind her, the projected headline echoed how he felt. *Shocker in New Starkham!*

"The same thing as you, apparently," he said. "Tricky. You've got your entire family freaking out. Your grandmother called this morning and told me what happened last night when you got home."

"She did?"

"She was worried about you."

"Gramma didn't want me involved." She blinked, completely closed up. "I had to throw her off."

"You should call her and tell her you're safe. Or maybe I should."

"Please . . . don't." She reached out for his arm, then stopped herself. "If I can figure out all this nonsense before she does, she won't get hurt. She shouldn't be worrying about cursed jawbones at her age."

Timothy sighed, knowing he was about to break his promise to Zilpha. He pulled up a chair next to her. "How did you figure out this place was here?"

"Got up early. Looked out my bedroom window. Saw the campus. Realized the answer was staring me in the face. Oh, and by the way," she said, "I'm doing this on my own."

"But . . ."

"I know I sound like a jerk," she said, "but after last night,

I realized that I need to do this alone, or not at all. This is about *my* family. You shouldn't be involved, Timothy."

It took him a moment to catch his breath. "Abigail, what I said to you on the bus was really unfair."

"You're right. It was. And that's fine," she answered, blushing and turning back to the screen, "but your apology doesn't change my mind. Besides, this is a small room, and your gym bag sorta stinks."

"Oh," said Timothy, getting up and backing toward the door. "Right. Sorry. I'll just . . . wait out here until you're done."

"Cool," she said, scrolling through the article on the machine.

At the doorway, Timothy couldn't help himself. "Abigail, please," he said. "I'm really sorry."

She turned to look at him. In the half-light, for just a moment, he could see something in her eyes, something that told him she was sorry too. "You already said that," she answered, then turned away.

Timothy sat at the bottom of the staircase just outside the microfiche room. The carpet was worn, its threads just barely covering a flight of wooden steps that led upward. Frustrated, Timothy pulled at the weave, loosening it further.

Fine, he thought. Be like that. At least I tried.

Timothy stood up and strolled through the last few rows

of books, but he and Abigail were losing precious time. What was she *doing* in there?

Moments later, distracted, he crept up the stairs. With each step, Timothy grew angrier. He'd only ever tried to be nice to this girl. Right now, she was being meaner than Stuart could ever imagine.

Timothy found himself standing in the middle of a dark landing. A black plastic tarp hung loosely from the ragged wallpaper near the top, covering part of the wall. Renovations? After a moment, Timothy pulled the tarp aside. Behind the black plastic, he found a dark gap, and then an older wall, a foot behind the first one. In the center of this second wall was a door with filthy pebbled glass, so it was impossible to see inside the room.

As Timothy stared at the dirty glass, he saw that there had once been words decaled that had since been scratched off.

Dropping his bag to the landing floor, he went limp. He grabbed on to the knob for support, reading again the impression of the scratched-away words.

DR. CHR TIAN H SSEL S–
PROFES OR OF H ST RY

30.

Timothy turned the knob and the latch clicked. The door wheezed open a crack. A sliver of darkness stared at him. Timothy took a step backward, trying to catch his breath. He glanced down the stairs, toward the main reading room. Daylight spilled across the floor. No one seemed to notice him.

Frances May had told him that this man had been a professor. According to Zilpha Kindred, Hesselius had done something bad and had been locked away. This room must have been the man's office. The door had been walled over, erased. Weird. Why would the college abandon an entire room?

Curious, Timothy nudged the door open. The hinges creaked quietly. He listened for any sound of movement. "Hello?" he whispered. After a few seconds of silence, he realized he was alone. He pushed the door open fully. The room was not as dark as it had first seemed. From the doorway, Timothy noticed small details: a thick oak desk, a green glass lamp, a wall of bookshelves filled with bell jars, academic volumes, and picture frames. Velvet moth-eaten curtains hung from the tall windows. Next to the windows, two cracked leather chairs stared at each other, like a pair of old gentlemen whose conversation had run out.

Abigail needed to know about this, but would she listen?

Tentatively, he stepped inside. He strolled through the chamber, feeling like a ghost, as if he'd accidentally stepped outside of time. Finally, he pulled the curtain away from one of the windows. Light flooded the room, dust erupted in a torrent of motes, and he was blinded. He shaded his eyes. He saw the glass top of the Husketomic Lighthouse across the river.

The room was both larger and more cluttered than it had first appeared. Two flags stood erect on either side of the window—one was the American flag; the other was a pale gray felt, embroidered with a white triangle of stars. Timothy lifted the second flag to see it more clearly. In the center, three hand-stitched words echoed the triangle:

RIGHTEOUSNESS, INTEGRITY, SACRIFICE.

What kind of flag was *this*?

The intense beam of light that flooded the room was at the perfect angle to illuminate a crooked frame hanging on the wall opposite the window. Timothy crept across the room and straightened the frame. Inside was an old photograph of the lighthouse, the Taft Bridge, and cliffs across the river. Faint pencil marked the matte-paper frame behind the glass. In old script, someone had written *Hesselius Illuminarium. 1940. A Light in the Darkness.*

Timothy gasped. His brother's mantra. Was this an example of Ben's Order in Chaos theory—literally, his Light in the Darkness—or was this just more coincidence? Either way, Timothy felt the need to look closer, as if he'd been *meant* to find this office.

Someone touched his shoulder, and Timothy spun. Behind him stood Ben, purple lips pulled back into an awful smile.

31.

Timothy tripped backward and was about to scream, "Get away from me!" when he heard Abigail's voice say, "Didn't mean to scare you." Suddenly, Ben flickered and disappeared. In his place stood Abigail.

Timothy blinked and exhaled. He slowly reached out and poked her shoulder. She was solid. Good. "You . . . shouldn't sneak up on people," he said, shaking the phantom from his mind's eye.

"I, uh, just wanted to let you know the microfiche machines are free," said Abigail, clutching a pile of papers. She eyed him suspiciously, then glanced at his bag on the floor near the open door. "I followed the chlorine smell. What is this place?" She reached out and touched the pane of glass where Dr. Hesselius's name had once been painted. "Oh my gosh," she whispered.

“His office,” said Timothy.

“You mean, it was right above my head the entire time?” Her face went pale.

Timothy nodded.

“But what’s with . . . ?” She gestured to the tarp.

Timothy shook his head. “I think . . .” He paused, unsure if Abigail would understand Ben’s Order-Chaos theory. “It’s complicated,” he answered. “The important thing is that we’re closer to an answer.” Abigail began backing away, crushing the papers against her chest. She looked like she had last night, just before she’d run away. “Oh, come on, Abigail, you can’t do this by yourself,” he said. She still seemed unsure. “Look around,” he added. “This isn’t *just* about your family.”

Abigail surveyed the room. After Timothy showed her the strange gray flag, she was confused too. Finally, he led her to the wall with the photo of the lighthouse.

As she examined the writing, he noticed another frame filled with old-fashioned baseball cards sitting on the bookshelf next to the wall. Names were printed on the cards underneath the players’ photos, but Timothy couldn’t read them through the thick layer of crud.

“Timothy, what’s—?”

“Hold on,” he whispered, leaning closer to the bookcase. He grabbed the frame from the shelf, cleaned the dust from the glass, then noticed three familiar names in the bottom right corner. In order, they were the men who played second, first, and third bases on this team. He gasped.

"Tell me what's going on," said Abigail. "What are you looking at?"

Timothy showed her.

"Baseball cards?" she said, skeptically. "So what? According to the articles I found, Dr. Hesselius was a well-known collector of Americana. As a historian, that was one of his special interests."

Timothy smiled. "Nothing more American than baseball, is there?" he said. "Check out the bottom." When Abigail read the names, she dropped the papers she'd been holding. As she bent down to retrieve them, Timothy looked closer at the portraits and whispered, "Carlton Quigley. Bucky Jenkins. And Mr. Leroy 'Two Fingers' Fromm."

32.

A few minutes later, they were seated in the dusty leather chairs. Abigail examined the framed collection of baseball cards, then picked at the frame's backboard, which was held in place by several stubborn nails. Timothy flipped through the articles she had printed. Headlines leapt out at him. *Confession! Kidnapping Tragedy! Professor Tied to Evil Cult!* On one page, Timothy thought he saw a photograph of Abigail herself, but realized it was a picture of her grandmother. *Zilpha Kindred, Hero,* read the caption.

Timothy glanced at Abigail, who had managed to pry away one of the frame's rear prongs. "What are you doing?"

"These cards have secrets," she said. "Can't learn them if they're locked away."

"Speaking of secrets," he said, as she continued to pick at

another stubborn nail, "what did you find? There's too much here to go through." Abigail sighed. Timothy chuckled in disbelief. "You *still* don't want to talk? Fine, then I will."

Timothy told Abigail about seeing Ben the night before. Abigail listened, but she did not seem as astounded as he expected her to be. She hung her head and wouldn't look at him. Back to her old tricks, he thought, but when she finally began her own story, he changed his mind.

"Last night," Abigail began, "the Nightmarys came back."

"Oh," he whispered. Zilpha hadn't told him this part.

"I'd been so upset by what had happened earlier—you know . . . on the bus—that after I lay down on the couch and they showed up, I finally followed them."

"After everything we've been through?" said Timothy. "How? Why?"

Abigail pulled her hair away from her face and leaned back into the chair. "I didn't plan on it. They wore me down. I felt like I was sleepwalking down the hallway, but I knew I was awake, and I couldn't stop or even scream. Something inside me actually wanted to follow them, telling me that I deserved whatever happened next.

"Gramma found me at the elevator. I told her everything. I promised her I'd stay out of it, but you know that's impossible now. I won't see her get hurt. This morning, I wrote a note that I was going back to New Jersey. I snuck out early so no one could stop me. I came here to the campus. Like I said downstairs, I didn't want *you* involved, because I don't want you to get hurt either. And here we are, together again."

Silence filled the room.

Finally, Timothy said, "But I'm a part of this now. You know that. I need answers as much as you do."

"You're right, Timothy," said Abigail, smiling weakly. "We are really close to figuring out something huge."

"Dr. Hesselius is behind all of this."

Abigail nodded, still pulling at the frame. "But there's just one problem."

"What's that?"

She glanced up. "Dr. Hesselius is dead." She took the papers from Timothy. Flipping through them, she stopped at an article near the back of the packet. *Mad Doc Hangs,* read the headline.

"That's what Zilpha told me. He was executed?"

"No," said Abigail. "He did it in his cell a few years after the trial. Here, start at the beginning." She shuffled through the pages again. "We've got a nearly complete biography here. The *New Starkham Record* has snippets of Dr. Hesselius's career going back to the early nineteen twenties."

"What does it say?"

"Well, here's a blurb from when New Starkham's history department hired him," said Abigail, perusing the article.

"His family was really rich. He played baseball at his Ivy League school. He was a private in the army during World War One. The article goes on, stating his specialties in ancient civilizations, particularly the histories of warfare and engineering, which he taught here."

"Sounds normal for a professorish type of person," said Timothy. "But where's the 'bad' part?"

"This is only the first article. There's tons more," she said. She held up another page. "He was really generous. He gave to all sorts of foundations—museums, sports programs, schools. He was involved in local elections and helped his favorite candidates win. He donated money to build that lighthouse across the river and even helped design it. People here seemed to love him."

"I'm still not hearing the 'bad,' " said Timothy.

"That's because there's not much 'bad' to say about him," said Abigail, looking up. "Not yet." She shuffled some more pages. "Here's his marriage notice. And here's a small piece about the birth of twins."

"He had kids?"

"Two boys," said Abigail. "He lost one of them in World War Two. A bomb . . ." Abigail stopped.

It took Timothy several seconds to realize why she didn't finish her sentence. Timothy spent several seconds forcing Ben's zombie face out of his head. He leaned forward. "And?"

"The other one never served. Didn't pass the medical

exam, I think. The death of his son seems to have been the turning point," said Abigail. "Dr. Hesselius was devastated. He'd been proud to send one of them to fight for his country, just like he had in the first war. He never expected . . ." She blinked and pressed her lips together.

"Go on," he said.

"Let's see. Here, from the college paper, *History Professor*

Takes Leave of Absence." She read through the page quickly. "The article hints at some sort of breakdown. Exhaustion. Psychiatric treatment. It doesn't go into details." She shrugged. "There's no other mention of him until a few years later." She flipped through more pages. "After the war ended, he was back . . ."

Timothy took a deep breath. "Here comes the 'bad'?"

Abigail nodded. "*Local Professor Questioned in Disappearance of Child,*" she read. "From an article in the *New Starkham Record.*" She handed the page to Timothy, so he could read it.

July 7, 1946 – New Starkham – Dr. Christian Hesselius, a local professor, is being questioned by police about the July 4 disappearance of 14-year-old Delia Benson of Dreyer Street. Zilpha Kindred, a student at Thomas Jefferson High School, brought to the authorities' attention a photo she had taken at the city's annual Independence Day Parade. The blurry image appears to show the

> professor with Miss Benson in a Johnson Street alleyway. According to Miss Kindred, "Delia was interviewing the crowd, while I took pictures for the first issue of the school paper. My camera captured what my own eyes did not." Ms. Benson's younger sister, Emma, who was marching in the parade, also places Hesselius at the scene. She boldly stated, "I will testify. Anything to find my sister." Dr. Hesselius has taught at New Starkham College for over twenty years. He has yet to be charged with any crime.

Timothy looked up from the page. "That is really freaky. Your poor grandmother."

"I know," said Abigail, shaking her head. "But that's nothing compared to the article a couple days later." She handed him another page. *"Hesselius Charged with Kidnapping,"* she said. "Formal charges were made and bail was set really high. He confessed to kidnapping Delia a few days after that, but he refused to say where he'd taken her and what he'd done to her."

Timothy shuddered. The office walls encroached, as if the room itself was listening. "Why did he confess if he wasn't going to tell anyone where she was?"

"According to the article," said Abigail, scanning the page, "he knew the evidence was against him, but he also said Delia wasn't ready yet."

"Wasn't ready for what?"

"It's kind of crazy. According to court transcripts, he'd locked her away as a sacrifice to . . ." Abigail shook her head. "The Daughter of Chaos?"

Timothy blinked. "What the hell is that supposed to mean?"

"The paper says Hesselius had uncovered an ancient Scandinavian tribal sect that worshipped obscure gods, goddesses, giants, and spirits. They believed they could harness ancient magic during their rituals using strange metals."

"The Daughter of Chaos . . . Like what the placard at the museum said." Timothy gasped. "Abigail, Zilpha said after today, all this will be over. Do you think she was at the museum that day looking for the jawbone?"

Abigail nodded. "The Daughter of Chaos was one of the obscure goddesses worshipped by the sect. They believed that if you appeased her, she gave you great powers."

This was starting to sound familiar. Zilpha Kindred's uncle hadn't strayed very far from the headlines for the plot of *The Clue of the Incomplete Corpse*. "Such as?"

"Such as the ability to control fear," said Abigail.

"And . . . how would they appease this goddess?" he asked, though he felt like he already knew the answer.

"The sect built temples at the locations of great natural 'chaos.' Waterfalls. Chasms. Caves. Volcanoes. The tribe would place a corpse inside the temple. A chip of the tribe's sacred metal was inserted into a tooth socket of the corpse. This metal 'tooth' infused the corpse with a connection to the spirit of the goddess. Then a ritual was performed to 'charge' the tooth. A person, often an enemy of the tribe, was locked in the temple with the corpse as a sacrifice. Supposedly, at the full moon, the corpse rose, all vampirelike, and drained the life essence of her victim. With the goddess satisfied and the metal charged, the corpse would again fall into slumber."

"So Delia was the . . . sacrifice?" said Timothy, feeling sick. "The *battery*?"

Abigail nodded again. "Once the tooth was charged, the cult would remove the jawbone from the goddess corpse. From here on, the story pretty much mirrors what we read about my great-uncle's book. Whoever holds the jawbone controls the Daughter of Chaos's power."

"The *fear* thing?"

"Right."

"The placard at the museum said you needed to grasp the jawbone and speak the victim's name, and then the soul's charge inside the metal tooth would place a curse on the victim. The user could control the victim by psychically manipulating what they were afraid of." Timothy paused. "So what did Doctor Crazy plan on using it for?"

Abigail took a deep breath. "Revenge."

"On who?"

"The people he blamed for his son's death. Nazis? I don't know. He never really said."

Timothy glanced around the room. Certain objects were now filled with new meaning: the photographs, the flags, even the baseball-card collection. "So the jawbone was a weapon."

"Delia, he claimed, was his first experiment. Hesselius never revealed where he'd taken her. Once he realized that people thought he was totally insane, he never spoke about the ancient sect again. At least not publicly. Then, a few years later, he was gone."

"So that's that?" asked Timothy. "The end?"

Abigail raised her hands, gesturing to the room. "Obviously not."

"You mean . . . ?"

"What you said on the bus last night, Timothy . . . You were right. All of this . . . *everything* that has happened . . . It all makes sense. Someone has that jawbone and has been using it against us."

"Why?" said Timothy. "What did *we* do?"

Abigail closed her eyes and shook her head. "I don't know."

Timothy stood up, "But, Abigail, if the jawbone is a weapon, then we have our defense." He wandered to the back of the chair, trying to sort out the situation. She stared at him quizzically. "Your Nightmarys. Stuart's monster. All of it. Fear. It's not real."

"We don't *know* that," said Abigail. "It all seems pretty real!"

Timothy paused to think. "Well, what do we know? Stuart ended up in the hospital. Mr. Crane called me about the specimen jars. You nearly followed those girls out into the rain. . . . Maybe it doesn't matter what's real. Maybe all that matters is *what we believe*? The jawbone controls fear. And fear controls us."

"Yes!" Abigail said. "If my grandmother hadn't shown up at the elevators when she did last night, I'd be in big trouble right about now. It's *not* the Nightmarys who want me to follow them. It's someone else. If the jawbone gives the user the ability to read minds, he's controlling my fear of them to get me where he wants me."

"Where would that be?" said Timothy.

Abigail shook her head. "My grandmother said Hesselius wrote her a letter from his cell, promising that someday, she would pay for telling on him."

"Pay how?"

A cold draft swept past them. The floor creaked slightly. Timothy and Abigail both spun. The plastic tarp outside made a crinkling sound. A tall silhouette stood framed in the opening. Timothy felt the room start to spin. He clutched the back of the leather chair, as Abigail leapt to her feet. A deep voice said, "What are you doing in here?"

33.

"We were—" Timothy began, but the man interrupted with a wave of his hand.

"Save it." He stepped inside. His dark hair and beard were salted with white. He wore black jeans, an untucked dress shirt, and a dark blazer. "Wendy told me she gave a couple of visitor passes to some middle-school students earlier this morning. I didn't see anyone downstairs who fit that description, so I thought I'd do a little exploring, and what do I find?" The man smiled, revealing crooked yellow teeth. "Trespassers."

"Um, sir?" Timothy raised his hand. "Technically, we're not trespassing. There wasn't a keep-out sign on the door."

"I guess common sense is a difficult concept for today's youth," said the man. "Come on. Time to go."

"We're wicked sorry," said Timothy, heading toward the door. "We didn't mean any harm."

"Yeah, totally no harm meant," Abigail whispered, trailing behind him.

When they reached the door, the man stopped Abigail. "What's this?" he said, glancing at the framed baseball cards.

"Oh, that's, um . . . ," said Abigail, but she wasn't quick enough.

The man took the frame from her. "I recall these sitting in front of the safe on that bookshelf over there. At least, that's where they were the last time I checked."

The safe? thought Timothy. What safe? He glanced at Abigail. She looked as shocked as he was. The man brushed past them, crossed through the room, and slid open a small wood panel in the bookshelf. Inside the cupboard was a metal door, a combination lock plugged into its center. "Locked," said the man, closing the door and replacing the frame. "Strange, if you ask me," he continued, "but then again, in my opinion, this whole situation is strange. Beyond strange." The man ushered Timothy and Abigail out the door, past the plastic curtain, and onto the landing. "You'd think after almost fifty years, the college would have left this room alone," said the man. "They were the ones who put up this wall in the first place. But no. Now we need space. Space! *We cannot waste the space!* And *I* have to deal with the mess."

"You mean," Abigail said, following the man down the stairs, "the *college* put up that wall?"

"One of the old librarians asked them to," said the man. "Sealed that office right up."

"But why?" said Timothy.

Once they reached the bottom of the stairs, the man stopped and turned around. "And I'd be telling you for what reason?" He squinted at them.

"Actually," said Abigail, "it's kind of weird, but we're here doing research about the man who used that office."

"Dr. Hesselius?" said the man. Surprised, the kids nodded. Abigail pulled the microfiche pages from under her arm and handed them to him. The man flipped through them with a curious expression. "Why would you want to know about him?"

A few minutes later, Timothy and Abigail were behind the front desk, helping the man, who'd introduced himself as Gavin Engstrom, load heavy books onto a wobbly cart. Abigail had convinced Gavin to tell them the history of Hesselius's strange office in exchange for a round of reshelving. He'd sent the blond assistant away for the moment.

Gavin leaned against the desk and folded his arms. "The plans began last year when someone up in the admissions building noticed the window anomaly." Both Abigail and Timothy stared at him. "There were more windows outside than we could account for on the inside," Gavin continued. "The Office of Building and Development soon rediscovered the room at the top of the stairs. As I was saying, space is quite a commodity at this institution. Of course, I've been fully aware of the room ever since I started here. After the library erected the wall, the abandoned office was secret staff knowledge, passed down through these last few generations, like an heirloom. I had come to the conclusion that the room had actually become invisible."

Timothy snickered. "Well, that's just . . . ," he began. Just what? Silly? A moment later, Timothy realized it wasn't silly. After everything he'd just learned, it was actually really creepy.

"I'm assuming you know a bit about the former occupant," Gavin went on, nodding at the pages Abigail had stacked on the book cart. "Scary story, right?" Abigail and Timothy nodded. "Supposedly, the librarians at the time knew Hesselius pretty well. They liked him. Early on, during the trial, there had been talk about whether or not Hesselius might return, so they saved his office for him, just the way he left it. But after the government put him away, no one wanted to go in there. With all the talk, people didn't know what to believe. I think it was . . . Percival Ankh, the head librarian at the time, who locked up the office. And so it remained, for several years, a closed door," said Gavin. "Hesselius died. People said they heard noises in there. Rumors of voices. Cults. Dark magic. No one even used that staircase anymore. Creepy.

Mr. Ankh was a superstitious man. I'm pretty sure it was his idea to seal up the room behind the wall too."

"Did people think Hesselius's ghost was in there?" Timothy asked. "Did you ever see anything?"

"Me?" Gavin laughed. "No. I'm not the *seeing* kind."

Abigail bumped into the cart. It squeaked. "Upstairs, you seemed a little freaked out."

"Well, yes, I was nervous," Gavin said. "I heard *your* voices. I didn't expect to find a couple of kids up there gathering dust."

"Then why'd you make us give back that frame?" said Timothy.

Gavin laughed. "You wanna know why?" he asked. "First of all, it didn't belong to you. Second of all . . . it didn't belong to you!"

"Then it's not *cursed* or anything?" Timothy blushed.

"It very well may be, if you believe in curses," said Gavin, "but that's not my concern. Nothing can leave that room. You see, there's a lawsuit. Turns out, news of the room's discovery got back to Dr. Hesselius's relatives. They insist everything in that room belongs to them. No one's supposed to touch it until the college settles the issue."

"Who are his relatives?" said Abigail.

"His son, specifically," said Gavin. "A sweet old guy who still lives in New Starkham. I don't blame him for trying, the economy being what it is."

"You've met him?" said Timothy.

"Sure," said Gavin. "Came by the library a couple months ago. He hobbled up those stairs himself. Technically, he wasn't allowed, but I gave him some time to look around. Unlike *some* people I know, he left without touching a thing. I actually hope he gets everything he wants, though most of what's left in there is worthless, in my opinion. Still, I couldn't help feeling sorry for the guy. Losing his father the way he did."

"You mean, his father, the *child snatcher*?" said Abigail, tossing a book onto the cart.

"Hey, careful with that," said Gavin. He sighed. "Please. You know what I mean. He lost his twin brother too. Imagine how you would have felt if you were him."

"I don't think I really want to," said Abigail quietly, "but thanks anyway."

Gavin stared at her for several seconds, then shrugged. "People don't inherit the sins of their parents."

"Thank God," said Timothy and Abigail at the same time.

"Let's go," said the librarian. "Enough chat." He pushed the cart from behind the desk toward the bookshelves. The squeaky wheel echoed through the large room. "More action."

Moments later, Timothy followed Abigail into the Ancient Religions section. "We've got to get back up there."

"Where?" said Abigail. "The office?"

"That hidden safe," said Timothy. "The baseball-card

frame was right in front of it. It's gotta be a clue. We should check it out." He pulled a book from the cart, matched up the number on the spine, and shoved it into its place on the shelf. "Besides, after everything we've been through, there's no way I'm leaving those cards up there. I don't care if Gavin tries to stop us. I'd be willing to do some evasive action to get past him. Whenever we play basketball in gym class, I play pretty good offense."

"That won't be necessary," said Abigail, lifting another book from the cart.

Timothy shook his head. "What do you mean, not necessary?"

Abigail placed her book on the shelf. "The evasive action already happened, silly." She reached into her back pocket. "I doubt we can get back up there without being noticed, but at least we've got these." When she pulled out the three baseball cards, Timothy had to cover his mouth to keep from whooping. She held her finger up to her mouth and said, "Shhh."

34.

They finished shelving the books and returned the cart to the front desk, where Gavin was hunched over some paperwork.

"Excuse me one last time?" said Abigail. "Say we wanted to . . . find Dr. Hesselius's son?"

Gavin looked up, perturbed. "I'll ask again," he said. "Why should I be telling you this?" With a tiny smile, Abigail simply waved the microfiche printouts. Gavin rolled his eyes. "Research. Right." He sighed. "I think I have his contact information in my office. Just a second," he said. He went through a door behind the front desk. Moments later, he returned with a small white notecard, which he handed to Abigail. "This is all I have. I'm only doing this so you'll leave me alone and never come back here, at least until the semester is over." He glared at her. "Deal?"

"Yeah, sure. Thanks a lot," she added quickly.

The two kids casually walked out the library's front door. By the time they reached the bottom step, they were at a near sprint. They ran, sticking to the campus paths until they found the quad. Hunched over, Timothy stopped, trying to catch his breath. Abigail gasped, hugged the microfiche pages to her chest, then glanced over her shoulder up the hill. "Why were we running like that?" she asked.

"I don't know," said Timothy. "I was following you. I guess I thought we should get out of there before he took the notecard back. What'd he write on it anyway?"

Abigail had clenched the card in her fist. She opened her hand, turned the card over, and said, "Jack."

Timothy paused. "Jack? As in *jack squat*? As in *nothing*?"

"Jack . . . as in that's the old man's name. Hesselius's son," said Abigail, showing Timothy the card. "He wrote his address too."

"Ash Tree Lane?" Timothy read. "That's just a few blocks from my house."

"Cool," said Abigail, "so you can lead the way."

"Wait," said Timothy, handing the card back to her. "You actually want to go to the house?"

"What else did you have in mind for the afternoon? A game of Parcheesi with my grandmother?" said Abigail. "This guy has answers. He's got to know what's going on. Maybe he can tell us some more about his father. We can ask him about the baseball cards and the safe. Maybe he'll tell us what's in it."

"Yeah, sure." Timothy nodded. "Or maybe he can *kill* us."

Abigail smacked his arm. "He's old. What can he do?"

"You don't know how old he is," said Timothy.

"What are you worried about?" said Abigail. "Gavin said he 'hobbled.' I don't think someone who hobbles has enough strength to hurt us."

Timothy lowered his voice, like a television announcer, and answered, "She said as he whacked her with his sword cane."

"People don't inherit the sins of their parents," said Abigail. "That's what Gavin said."

"Yeah, but—"

"If we don't check out this address, we've hit a dead end. You can either come with me, or you can stand here admiring the view." She gestured toward the river. The lighthouse had fallen under the bridge's shadow, as the sun had now moved halfway across the sky. The wind off the water was chilly. Timothy's stomach growled. The campus was quiet, and they had nowhere else to go.

He figured they could stop by the old man's house, ring his doorbell, at least check the place out. Maybe this Jack guy wasn't home. Even if he was home, he might not know *jack*. They wouldn't know until they tried.

"Hold on," said Timothy, racing up the Dragon Stairs after Abigail. "I can't keep up with you."

"You? Mr. Swim Team can't keep up with a *girl*?" Abigail

called over her shoulder, teasing him. The rolled-up microfiche copies wagged from the back pocket of her jeans. Timothy laughed, which slowed him down even more, but then he glanced at the green paint on the wall, thought of the dragon's eyes, and stepped up his pace.

"The house isn't going anywhere," said Timothy.

"It's not the house I'm worried about," she said over her shoulder. "Do you believe in ghosts?"

"I've never really thought about it."

"Gramma thinks this is all about her, and she's going to try and stop it. Hesselius promised to return someday. Get his revenge on the little girl who told. After everything we learned at the library, I'm beginning to think maybe she's on to something."

"You think Hesselius's *ghost* has that jawbone thing?"

"Maybe. If that's even possible. I don't know what to think. All I know is I've got to keep Gramma safe."

35.

The house sat on Ash Tree Lane's last plot of land before the road became woods. A dead-end street. Of course.

"I've been here before," said Timothy, standing with Abigail on the opposite sidewalk. The cement beneath his feet was cracked. "Stuart and me used to come up here sometimes," he continued. "We'd play catch in the street, because we didn't have to worry about traffic. We always thought this house was empty."

"Maybe it was then," said Abigail, "but it's not now."

The house across the street was three stories tall—maybe a hundred fifty years old. Its white paint was chipped and, in some places, peeling in long, thin strips. Four massive wood columns stretched from the stone foundation to the sharp-peaked, triangular roof. Above the deep porch, a small octagonal window stared out over the rest of the neighborhood.

The remaining windows, four across each subsequent floor, were darkened. Dangling from the high porch roof, a long black chain swung in the breeze like a hypnotist's watch. From the end of the chain, a box lamp glowed dimly, defying the afternoon light.

"Yeah," said Timothy. "Looks like someone's home."

A jumble of early-spring weeds filled the deep yard behind the white fence, which separated the house from the street. A weeping willow brushed budding limbs against the right side of the porch. Around the left corner, an ancient black Mercedes was parked in front of a detached, barnlike garage.

Abigail stepped off the curb and started toward the house.

"Wait," said Timothy. "What's our plan?" Abigail shrugged and kept walking. He stayed where he was. "But what if he's a psycho? What if he tries to kill us?"

"We're just going to ask him some questions. It'll be quick," said Abigail. "Besides, at this point, I'm almost positive that whatever *is* trying to hurt us isn't human. Hesselius is dead, remember?"

"And that's a *good* thing?" he asked. A vengeful ghost? It seemed so silly. But then, life *had* become quite silly lately, hadn't it? "How are we supposed to stop a . . . ghost?"

"Maybe its son will know," she answered, brushing her short black hair off her forehead. Timothy tripped after her.

Abigail swung open the garden gate. They climbed the front steps. Abigail stuck out her finger and pressed the doorbell.

Deep inside the house, a buzzer rattled. It was a shocking sound, like a joke-shop handshake trick. After several seconds, they heard someone approach the front door. The doorknob turned, and the door opened. Standing just inside, a stooped man with gnarled knuckles grasped the handles of a silver walker. He seemed barely able to lift his head but managed to look at them with curious eyes. His distorted pupils seemed to spill into the ice-blue rings of his irises. The sight of the man's grandfatherly outfit—gray slacks, a stained white T-shirt, and fuzzy gray slippers—was a relief. Behind him, the house was filled with daylight. Inside the foyer, a large staircase wound upward to several landings.

"Can I help you?" said the old man, his voice shaking. He managed to smile, looking happy at the prospect of visitors, even if he did not recognize them.

Timothy nudged Abigail. She stepped forward. "Are you . . . Jack?"

"Jack?" said the man, amused. "Well, yes, I suppose some people call me that."

"We're looking for the son of Christian Hesselius," said Timothy.

The man raised his head, which trembled on his weak neck, and looked at them more closely. "Well, then . . . you've found him."

"We got your name and address from Gavin Engstrom at the college library," said Abigail. "Do you mind if we ask you some questions?"

The man seemed confused. "Is this about my father's office? Because my lawyer told me . . ."

"No, it's not . . . entirely," said Abigail. She cleared her throat. "We just wanted to talk to you about . . . the past."

"The past?" said the old man. His eyes darted between Timothy and Abigail. "Most kids your age aren't interested in talking about stuff like that."

"We're sorry to bother you," Timothy said, "but it's important."

"Ah, well, if it's *important,*" the man answered, teasing. He was silent for several seconds. Finally, he moved his walker out of the way and motioned for them to come inside. "Can I get you something to drink? Eat?" He led them through a doorway into the kitchen. "Sorry this place is such a mess. The visiting nurse doesn't work weekends, and even though it's not in her job description, she usually helps me clean up after myself. I've never been very good at that. Not even when I could lift more than a couple of books at a time." Across the room, his walker bumped into the oven. He glanced at the kids, who stood in the doorway. "So what'll it be?"

Timothy *was* hungry, but he knew that wasn't what they'd come for. Besides, this place didn't smell very good.

"Nothing for me, thanks," said Abigail.

"Please. At least sit down. I get nervous when people stand in doorways."

The kids came inside and stood next to the table. Jack waited several uncomfortable seconds, until they'd both pulled out chairs and sat down. "So . . . the past," he said. "What about it?"

Timothy glanced at Abigail. He couldn't think of anything intelligent to say. He hadn't thought this far ahead. Had she?

"Your father," said Abigail. "How well did you know him?"

Jack leaned against the oven, facing them directly. "As well as any son knows his parent, I suppose." When Abigail didn't immediately answer, he continued, "I think I understand what this is about."

"You do?" Timothy asked.

"You've heard the old stories," Jack suggested simply. "You want to know if they're true."

"The old stories?" said Abigail.

"This city has tried to erase his legacy, both good and bad," said Jack. "Over the years, people have often sought answers from me. In all honesty, when it comes to my father, I have no answers. I only have my opinion, and that is: my father was a good man . . . despite the evidence." He smiled. "That's *my* story and I'm sticking to it." The way Jack spoke reminded Timothy of someone reading a script, as if the old man didn't believe his own words.

"How long have you lived in this house?" Timothy asked. "I thought this place was empty."

"Oh, several months now. I'd been away from New Starkham for quite a while. Something brought me back, I guess. Nostalgia? I don't know. When you're my age, you don't have too many friends left in the world. You return to your roots. Either that or move to Florida. And I hate Florida."

Jack choked out a laugh. "*There's* one thing I can thank my daddy for: imprinting New Starkham in my brain. I've never forgotten this place or its people. I suppose you might say it's all part of me now." He pointed at them, his hand shaking. "You just wait. In sixty years, we'll see where you end up. Tell me if I'm right."

"But you'll be . . . ," Timothy began, before stopping and turning bright red. Abigail glared at him.

"What?" said Jack. He laughed again. "Dead? Well . . . that's probably true."

Abigail stood up. "Mr. Hesselius . . ." Timothy's nerves suddenly tied themselves up again. "We're here because we're trying to find out what happened when your father was . . . sent away. We spent the morning at the college library researching as much as possible about him. Timothy accidentally stumbled upon his old office. Gavin, the librarian, said he'd shown you around the place a couple of months ago. Is that true?"

The old man was quiet for several seconds. Timothy

could hear his own heartbeat drumming in his ears. Way to get right to the point, Abigail, he thought.

"Now, now," said Jack, impressed, glancing at Timothy. "You've got yourself a sassy girlfriend."

"She's not my—" Timothy started, but Jack interrupted.

"It's true. I read in the papers about the reappearance of my father's belongings." He paused. "Why are you so interested? What's so important that you'd spend your Saturday morning at the library?"

"It's hard to explain," said Timothy.

"I really shouldn't talk about it. My lawyer . . ."

"Mr. Hesselius—" Abigail said.

"Please, Hesselius was my father," said the old man. "I'm Jack." He sighed and nodded. "To answer your question, yes, the librarian was kind enough to allow me access to the room."

Abigail leaned forward. "Did you find anything important?" she said slowly, as if her questions might scare him away. "Anything your father wouldn't have wanted anyone to know about?"

Jack snorted in surprise. "What are you getting at?"

Abigail started to reach into her back pocket. Timothy's mouth went dry. She pulled out the three baseball cards. Timothy clutched at the kitchen table. "Do these look familiar?" She got up and crossed to the oven.

"Where did you get . . . ?" Jack was stunned. "Did you

take those from the office?" Without hesitation, Abigail handed the cards to the old man.

"Not to keep," she said. "Just for . . . reference."

Jack's hands shook as he examined the players' faces. "Carlton Quigley. Bucky Jenkins. Leroy Fromm." He looked up. "The Diamond Stars. These guys were Daddy's favorites. He used to take me to games in Boston. I actually saw them play. These cards were very important to him. His pride and joy. I could never forget these," he said, his voice shaking with emotion. "Thank you for bringing them back to me."

Very quietly, Abigail answered, "You're welcome."

Jack's reaction to the cards made Timothy feel safe again. The old man looked truly happy. Timothy stood up and said, "The cards were in a frame. The frame blocked a safe built into a bookshelf. Gavin said the safe was locked."

Jack smiled. "Until *I* got there, it was," he said. Abigail glanced at Timothy, confused. "These cards are more than just cards. They're a clue my father left me a long time ago. It took me forever to figure it out. But the discovery of that room in the library certainly helped. I never even knew about it until I read about it. Pity they kept it sealed up all these years. So much wasted time."

"A clue?" said Timothy. "What kind of clue?"

"When I saw the frame, I was able to finally figure it out," said the old man. "Each player has a number on his jersey.

First, second, third base. Jenkins, Quigley, Fromm. The safe's combination."

Timothy tried to keep his voice even as he said, "So the safe *wasn't* empty?"

"Of course, my lawyer would kill me for telling this to anyone. . . . But you kids look like you can keep a secret," Jack whispered. "Am I right?" Without hesitation, Timothy and Abigail both nodded. "It was my father's journal," he added.

"Your father's journal was in the safe?" said Abigail.

"I slipped it into my coat pocket when that librarian wasn't looking," said Jack. "No one ever suspects the old man." He winked. "We get away with so much."

"What was in the journal?" Timothy asked.

"Proof," said Jack simply. "That my father was as human as the next. He was no monster. He loved me. He was distraught about Fred, my twin brother, who was killed in the war. I didn't serve. I'm not yellow or anything. Got the flat feet. It was a difficult time for me back then. People can be cruel." He shuddered, then continued. "The book was filled with pages upon pages of how much my brother and I meant to him, how much he missed Fred, what he would give if only he could have changed things." The old man stared at the floor. "I would have done anything to make him happy again. I've spent most of my life following in his footsteps. Studying what he studied. Learning what he knew. Finding that journal changed everything. . . ."

"The journal didn't mention anything else?" asked Abigail. Timothy knew what she wanted to ask. But how could they possibly bring up the Chaos Tribe, the trial, and Delia's resting place without seeming crazy themselves, or at least totally insensitive?

"See it for yourself," said Jack, grappling his walker's handles and shuffling the metal frame toward the kitchen door. "I think Jenny, my nurse, put the book in the upstairs office. I can't make the stairs, but you're welcome to go find it."

"O-Okay," said Abigail. She glanced at Timothy. He nodded. Maybe there was something in the journal that could take them to the next step.

Jack led the kids back into the foyer. He pointed up the stairs. "All the way to the top. Door's the only one in the hallway. I think the book is on the desk near the window. Bring it down, would you? I'd like to look at it again myself."

Together, Abigail and Timothy climbed the wide staircase. Each step creaked. At the first landing, an entry led to a short hall lined with closed doors. Timothy glanced up the next set of stairs. At the top landing, he could see the open door Jack had mentioned. It must lead to the room with the octagonal window over the porch. Timothy had a strange feeling. Why would an old man in Jack's condition purchase a tall house like this? Sure, Jack had mentioned that his nurse helped him out, but still, why not live in an apartment like Abigail's grandmother? He scrambled to follow Abigail up the stairs.

Jack called to them, "You make it?" At the top, Timothy glanced over the railing. The old man waved from the foyer. "It's a hike. I still haven't been up there," he said. "Stupid of me to buy a three-story house at my age, but I just fell in love with it. It's nice and quiet at the end of this street."

Timothy's stomach fluttered. Jack had just answered his question. Weird . . .

"Jenny said she put the book on the desk," Jack called, his voice growing faint as Timothy moved away from the railing and followed Abigail into the large empty room. "Do you see it?"

Bare wooden beams held up the violently pitched roof. The walls slanted all the way to the floor—raw, dusty planks. The desk sat underneath the window. Abigail stopped in front of it.

"Is it there?" Timothy whispered.

Abigail shook her head. She picked something up and turned around. In her hands was a familiar book. Timothy froze when he saw it; his feet stuck to the floor. It was not the notebook Jack had mentioned. He tried to reach out and take it from her, to see if his eyes were playing tricks, but he couldn't even do that. His arms went dead.

These cards are more than just cards. They're a clue my father left me a long time ago.

Looking at the cover of *The Clue of the Incomplete Corpse,* he wanted to start laughing, or crying, or shouting . . . anything to rid himself of this dreadful feeling. But he could barely breathe.

"That looks like the same copy I found in the museum," Timothy whispered. "Flip through it. Find 102, 149, and 203." Abigail opened the book. When she reached those pages, the faint pencil markings made everything clearer. "He said his father gave him a clue a long time ago. This book! Hesselius must have somehow gotten a copy. He wrote the names of his favorite players in it, expecting that his son would find the cards in his office. All Jack needed was their jersey numbers and field positions to figure out the combination. The thing was, Jack never found the office. He never learned what his father wanted him to know . . . until a couple of months ago."

"But then where's the journal . . . ?" Abigail asked, her voice trailing off as she glanced past Timothy's shoulder, her mouth dropping open.

Timothy spun toward the attic door. To his horror, Jack stood there wearing a strange smile. He was no longer hunched and wobbly; in fact, at his full height, he looked tall and strong. He held on to the doorknob, blocking the only way out. "Right here," he said. With his other hand, he revealed a small leather-bound book. "Full of secrets." Timothy felt Abigail grab his hand.

Jack reached into his pocket, pulling out the three baseball cards. "Earlier this week, after I dropped my book at the museum, I told you, Timothy, that *you shouldn't take things that don't belong to you.* You don't listen well."

Timothy felt his own skin shrink. It was him. The shadow man in the museum, and the locker room . . . maybe even the man he'd seen coming out of the Mayfair apartment building. This was the man with the jawbone, who had used Abigail's fear of the Nightmarys to make her believe this was all her fault. And he was no ghost.

"Don't worry, Abigail," said the old man. "I was never going to *hurt* you—a lesson I learned from my father. I'm not even going to touch you. Now that you know the truth, now that you fear the place where your end will come, the journey is inevitable. You'll probably just walk there yourself. Your fear will be your guide. And you won't have Granny to stop it from happening this time."

Keeping firm hold of her hand, Timothy stepped forward. "She has me," he said as loudly as he could manage, which wasn't very loudly at all.

"Oh, she has you, does she?" the old man asked, amused. "Well then, maybe you can go with her." He paused, considering them. "It's funny how things work out, don't you think?" He stepped backward into the hallway and closed the door. The lock turned. His footsteps creaked down the stairs.

36.

Timothy pounded on the door, and Abigail kicked at it. For almost a minute, they shouted for Jack to come back up and let them out, even as Timothy realized how foolish they were being. As if the old man would really change his mind. They leaned against the door, exhausted and frightened. Timothy spent several seconds trying not to say "I told you so."

Finally, Abigail turned to him and said, "Well, at least now we know."

"Now we know?" said Timothy. "Know what?" He was shocked that Abigail could sound so matter-of-fact.

"Everything, pretty much," she said. "And when you know stuff, you can use it against people."

Abigail laid the puzzle pieces out. Jack had said the cards were a clue his father had given him years ago. A code. Christian Hesselius had gotten his hands on a copy of the Zelda

Kite Mystery and used it to pass the code to his son. The writing in the book's margins might have been the last message Christian had ever given to his son. That was why it was so important that Jack retrieve the book from Timothy's gym locker.

"Right," said Timothy. "A few months ago, when the college opened the wall in the library, Jack learned that the code opened the safe in the bookshelf. He finally had access to his father's journal. The journal must have revealed the location of the jawbone."

"Well, we know it was at the museum," Abigail said. "Would Christian have donated it to such an obvious place?"

"Sometimes the hardest things to see are what's right in front of your face."

Abigail considered that for a few seconds. "Jack was at the museum during our field trip. Right? You saw him standing in that hallway. He watched everything that happened. Knowing I was angry with each of you, he cursed you and Stuart and Mr. Crane. Since he probably cursed me just after I moved here, he made me think that what was happening to all of you was my fault."

With all this cursing, the tooth's battery must be growing weak, thought Timothy.

Abigail continued. "The Nightmarys. If I didn't go with them, each of you would only get worse and worse. The Nightmarys never came to visit. Jack just wanted me to *think* they had." She paused. "What I don't understand is, how did he *know* the Nightmarys would have such power over me?"

"You said it yourself back at the library," Timothy answered. "The jawbone gives the user the ability to read the victim's mind. He got inside your head, influenced you, pushed the curse in a certain direction."

"Is Jack doing the same thing to Stuart and Mr. Crane?

And you too?"

"I don't know. Maybe he's not pushing *us* so much. The curse seems to work differently on different people, doesn't it? Maybe it depends on how you handle your fears? Maybe Stuart and Mr. Crane just freeze up, let it get the best of them? I know when I get scared, I have to do something about it. Maybe that's why I'm not stuck in a psycho ward."

Abigail lit up. "I can do that too," she said.

"What? Go to a psycho ward?"

"No, dummy. Handle it. Do something. Jack said something like 'I fear the place where my end will come.' And he's right. I do fear that. But how do I stop it from happening?"

"Maybe if we can figure out the place he's talking about, it won't seem so scary?"

Abigail closed her eyes and sighed. "I see a dark place. It's wet and cold and I'm alone." She looked at Timothy, distraught. "I don't know how to *not* be scared of it." Timothy took her hand, and she continued, "I wish we could ask my grandmother. She's always been so good at this kind of thing.

And this *is* all about her. Isn't it? That's why she kept calling it her mess. Jack wanted to hurt her, so he came after me."

"In the Zelda Kite books, though," said Timothy, "she always beat the bad guy in the end, right?"

"Yeah." Abigail's eyes blazed. She leapt to her feet. "I never got a chance to read those books, but I'm pretty sure she kicked his butt."

Outside, tires crunched on gravel and an engine turned off. Timothy and Abigail glanced at each other, then ran to the octagonal window. At the curb, a champagne-colored Cadillac had parked. As both the driver's- and passenger's-side doors opened, Abigail gasped. "What the . . . ?" she said.

"What's the matter?" said Timothy. "Who is it?"

Abigail turned to look at him. She wore a look of pure horror. "That's Georgia's car."

"Who's Georgia?" Timothy strained to see.

"My next-door neighbor," said Abigail. "Oh, no!" At that point, she didn't need to explain. Wearing a bright purple kimono, Zilpha Kindred had conspicuously climbed out of the passenger door and stood in the middle of Ash Tree Lane, staring curiously up at the house.

37.

"Your grandmother and Georgia?" said Timothy. "What are they doing here?"

"Who cares?" Abigail shouted. "They can help us." She reached across the desk and pounded on the window. "Gramma!" She screamed as loudly as she could. But the old woman didn't appear to notice. Abigail turned to Timothy. "Help me break this glass."

"With what?"

"Anything. It doesn't matter!" said Abigail, glancing around the room for some object to smash the window.

Timothy jumped onto the desk. He pulled his arm back, then punched his fist as hard as he could against the glass. An explosion of pain burst up his forearm. He fell off the desk and landed on his back in a cloud of dust. After a few seconds, he whispered, "Ouch."

"Are you okay?" said Abigail, scrambling over to him.

Timothy's hand was numb and warm, but he knew that soon the pain would begin. "No. I—I think I hurt it bad."

"We'll get you help," said Abigail, frantic. "But first we have to warn my grandmother." She glanced at the window. "Why didn't the freakin' glass break?"

Timothy struggled to sit. He leaned against the desk's thick wooden leg. "The curse. It makes our fears seem real, right? We're scared that your grandmother and Georgia won't hear us scream." He grunted as his fingers began to throb. "Pound on that window as hard as you want. We *can't* pound hard enough."

Abigail didn't listen. She leapt onto the desk and slammed both palms against the glass, again and again, but when the doorbell buzzed downstairs, she finally stopped. Abigail slumped off the desk and landed next to Timothy on the floor. "But she's *got* to hear us," she said, panting. She sounded defeated, tired, and in pain. "We have to warn her."

Timothy waved her quiet as she finally heard what he was hearing. The voices were muffled, but listening closely, Timothy could make out the conversation at the front door.

"Why, hello, Georgie," said the old man.

"Hi, Johnson," said Georgia. "I'd like you to meet my dear friend and neighbor, Zilpha Kindred."

"Johnson?" said Timothy. "I thought his name was Jack Hesselius."

"He must have changed it or something," said Abigail. "Didn't want to be associated with his dad?"

"Ah, the famous Johnson Harwood," said Abigail's grandmother. "It is truly a pleasure to finally make your acquaintance. Georgia has been singing your praises for months now. What a strange coincidence my needing your help like this."

"Gramma," Abigail whispered to no one in particular.

Timothy closed his eyes and leaned closer to the floor.

"Georgie'd been telling me we must meet, have dinner, something. But it never happened," said the old man jovially. "I hear you actually came to the museum looking for me," he continued, "but I wasn't around that day."

"He definitely *was* there that day," said Timothy. "Liar."

"He's Georgia's boyfriend?" said Abigail, in shock. "That's how he knows about me. Eww, that's so creepy."

"The museum must keep you quite busy," Zilpha's voice came through the floor. "Director is a big job, isn't it?"

"Never stops," said the old man.

Abigail grabbed Timothy's hand. "*He's* the museum director?"

Timothy nodded, enraptured by what he was learning. "That's why he was in the basement during the field trip. He works there. He was watching us. Learning."

"But I'm here now," Zilpha continued, "so we can chat and hopefully conduct the business I mentioned earlier."

"Ah," said the old man. "The jawbone."

"Yes," said Zilpha. "The *Record* mentioned it in that article about recent donations to the museum. It will be perfect for my project."

"Jawbone?" said Georgia. "What kind of jawbone?"

"An artifact," said the old man, "that once belonged to an ancient human. One of our more recent acquisitions."

"Recent acquisitions!" cried Timothy. "See? Christian *didn't* hide the jawbone at the museum. Since Jack is the museum director, he must have used his father's journal to locate the jawbone. Then *he* brought it to the museum."

"Why would he do that?" asked Abigail. Timothy shook his head.

"How morbid!" Georgia cried.

"It's not morbid. It's history." The old man forced a laugh. "I'd taken home the bone earlier this week to examine it more closely. Coincidentally, curious Mrs. Kindred, here, came to the museum looking for it. Come on in, and I'll tell you everything you need to know."

"Oh, I'm so pleased!" said Zilpha, her voice becoming clearer. She was now inside the foyer. "Maybe you'll let me get my hands on it. And do call me Zilpha."

Abigail and Timothy stared at each other in shock.

There was a pause. Then the old man said, "It's quite delicate, Zilpha."

"I understand," she answered. "I'll be gentle. Obtaining a

tactile sense of the object would be beneficial to the photo project I'm working on. If you don't mind, of course."

Timothy whispered, "Your grandmother knows he has the jawbone. She's trying to get hold of it."

"Does she know who he is?" asked Abigail.

"Doesn't seem like it."

"But what's she want with the jawbone? She's not going to

curse him with it."

There was silence downstairs. Then Jack, or Johnson, or whatever his name was, said, "Please have a seat in the living room. I'll be back shortly."

Abigail pounded on the floor and pressed her mouth up to a crack between the boards. "Gramma!" she called. Timothy pounded on the floor too.

Zilpha finally said, "Georgia, do you hear that?"

"Yes," said Georgia. "Must be the television upstairs? Johnson won't admit it, but he *is* hard of hearing." Timothy and Abigail looked at each other in frustration, then continued to shout. But Georgia went on, "Ooh, is that it?" Jack was back. "So small and disgusting. How old did you say the bone was, Johnson?"

"The tests indicate possibly thousands of years," said Jack. "That's why I must ask you to put on these gloves, Zilpha."

"He's just going to give it to her?" Timothy said.

"Like a doctor's office," Jack joked. No one laughed.

A few more seconds of silence; then he said, "And here you go. I hope this helps your photo—"

Georgia screamed.

The old man cried, "What are you doing?"

"I—I'm sorry," said Zilpha. "It slipped out of my hands."

"But, Zil, your shoe!" said Georgia. "You're stepping on it! Stop! You're crushing it!"

"Oh, my," said Zilpha dramatically. "I'm such a klutz. I'm *so* sorry, Mr. Harwood."

"Please!" said the old man, his voice stern. "Don't move! Maybe I can salvage some of it." After a moment, he screamed, "Wait!" He sounded pained. "Now you've pulverized it."

Abigail turned to Timothy, wearing an enormous smile of comprehension. "*That's* what she came for," said Timothy. "To destroy the jawbone and its link to the metal tooth."

"If she breaks the talisman, the curse will be broken too!" said Abigail. "I was so stupid. She promised me she would finish this herself."

"Maybe we should go?" suggested Georgia.

"That's a fantastic idea," said Jack. "I've got quite a mess to clean up."

"I'm so sorry, Mr. Harwood," said Zilpha. "I really didn't mean—"

"No!" said the old man. "Don't . . . touch . . . *anything*. . . ."

"I'm an old, clumsy woman," said Zilpha, her voice

moving directly below the floor now, back in the foyer. "I—I really didn't mean any harm."

"I'm sure you never do," said the old man. "But that doesn't help me *now,* does it?"

"I suppose not," said Zilpha. "Maybe I can pay for it?"

The old man laughed. "The artifact is irreplaceable. How much do you think something like this is worth? Believe me, the answer is not a sum total! I cannot simply send you a bill, Zelda!"

"It's . . . Zilpha," said Georgia quietly.

"Zelda, Zilpha!" said Jack. "Whatever! Just get out."

"Now, Johnson," said Georgia, distraught. "You're upset. We'll go. You drink some milk. Lie down. You'll feel better." The women were outside now, possibly on the porch. Timothy ran to the window, climbed onto the desk, and watched them make their way through the front garden and out the gate. All hope was leaving with them. Abigail stood silently beside him, watching them go. Downstairs, Jack started to chuckle.

38.

The light in the attic grew dim as the sun moved closer to the western horizon. Blue sky continued to stare at them through the octagonal window, but this clear weather was no comfort; in fact, it made things worse. Jack had left the house and driven away a while ago, leaving Timothy and Abigail alone to worry.

To kill time, Timothy examined the attic door once more. All he learned was that his hand still hurt. The door's hinges were tight, and the lock felt solid; then again, so had the window when he'd tried to break it. Timothy's gym bag was down in the kitchen, so the only weapon they had was Johnson Harwood's ratty copy of *The Clue of the Incomplete Corpse,* and only if the old man came back could they smack him with it.

"There's got to be some way out of here," said Timothy. When Abigail didn't answer, he looked at her sitting on the desk. She hung her head and hugged her rib cage. "Don't you think?" She remained silent. Timothy stood. "Come on," he said. "What happened to us being heroes?"

Abigail laughed, but it was not a happy sound.

"Are you worried that he went after your grandmother?" said Timothy. "Because I have a feeling she can take care of herself."

"Oh, you do?" said Abigail, tucking her chin closer to her chest. "Then why am I so freaked out?"

Timothy crossed the room. He took both of Abigail's hands into his own, as best he could. "Abigail," he whispered. "We can control it. That's why we're still okay. We are getting out of here, no matter what."

"No matter what?" she asked. Then, eyes wide, Abigail suddenly pulled away. "Shhh," she whispered. "And don't turn around." At her word, he froze, goose bumps embracing every inch of him. Then he heard a sound that made everything even worse. The door hinges squeaked, and he couldn't stop from spinning.

The door had opened a crack. Had it even been locked? The room was filled with violet haze—remnants of the light through the window—but in the darkest corners, thick layers of dirty cobwebs clung from the floor to the sloped walls, wavering in a slight draft.

"Were those there before?" Timothy whispered.

"What do you think?"

"I'm gonna go with . . . no?"

"How fast do you think we can make it to the door?" Abigail whispered.

"I'm not so sure I *want* to make it to the door now," said Timothy. "Something on the other side opened it."

"Yeah, but something on *this* side wants us to leave."

Timothy strained his eyes. Small dark shapes shifted beyond the webs, pulling the flimsy curtains away from the walls. Holes grew as the webs stretched to their breaking points. All at once, the dark shapes solidified, became small, childlike bodies. Two figures stepped through the webs, which clung to them like rotting veils. Mary Brown and Mary White? Abigail and Timothy screamed, clutching at each other.

The door swung open. Instead of a tall old man, another girl appeared in the doorway. Her face was a blur. She wore a dress similar to the others', made of dirty white cobwebs, rags, and lace, tied together with bits of string and knotted twine that dangled past her bare feet. Timothy choked out, "The Nightmarys?" Abigail did not answer, but instead grabbed his arm and stepped forward. None of the girls moved. "How come we're *both* seeing them now?"

"Maybe we're both scared of them now."

"Get out of here!" Timothy shouted at the girls. "Leave us alone!"

"Shhh," said the one in the doorway.

Abigail pulled him toward the door. The two figures in the shadows turned like clockwork to watch them move through the room. As Abigail slowly approached the girl who had opened the door, more and more of them appeared behind the patches of web, then stepped through. The room was suddenly crowded, and Timothy was getting claustrophobic.

"What . . . are . . . we . . . doing?" Timothy said through a clenched jaw.

"Getting out of here," Abigail whispered back.

When they were several feet away from the girl in the doorway, she stepped into the hall and held out her hand, as if welcoming them to their doom.

"Should we just walk by?" Timothy asked.

Abigail answered by pulling him forward. Timothy tried not to look as they crept past the creature. He sensed her watching him. Out of the corner of his eye, he could see her face shifting, dissolving, and reassembling behind the veil, unable to hold shape, like the figures behind the cobwebs had done before they'd emerged into the room.

Once on the landing, they tried to run toward the stairs, but Timothy lost Abigail's grip. When he turned around, he realized the figure in the doorway had stepped between them. Remembering how his hands had passed through zombie Ben last night, Timothy wondered how solid the apparitions actually were. He reached out for Abigail, but she slipped away from him. He stumbled, which gave the creature time to block

Abigail entirely. But he bolted at the phantom girl anyway. Before he made contact, the rest of the cobwebbed girls rushed through the attic toward the doorway, arms raised, hands reaching, fingers clutching, nails now sharp as talons.

Timothy froze as Abigail screamed, "Stop!" She panted. "They'll kill you. I know they will, because *I'm terrified* that they will." The Nightmarys paused, crowded at the attic door, watching him. *Were* they only an illusion? They looked so real.
"Timothy, run!" Abigail cried.

"I can't leave you here," he said.

The girl who was blocking Abigail stepped aside, revealing the small legion of specters waiting beyond the doorframe. The grotesque group broke forward, pushing through the door and onto the landing, immediately separating Timothy from Abigail. Now through their thin cobweb veils he could see their faces, but he couldn't comprehend what he was looking at, as if his brain wouldn't let him see. Words couldn't describe the horror he felt as they raced toward him.

"Get help!" Abigail cried. "Run!"

Inches away, the girls' claws reached for his throat. Timothy tripped backward down the stairs, caught the railing, and steadied himself. Taking three steps at a time, he made it to the next landing before turning around, but Abigail was gone. In her place, more and more of the wretched creatures streamed from the attic door, barreling down the stairs toward him.

The stairwell filled with the sound of strange chattering, unintelligible static, almost like birdsong, as the Nightmarys communicated to each other in their own secret language. Timothy fell through a doorway behind him: the hall with the closed doors. The mob swiftly approached. Timothy grabbed the nearest knob and turned it. The door swung outward, and he slipped inside a dark closet. He peered around the door but couldn't see the bottom of the stairs. The chattering came closer, and the floor began to shake as if a stampede of large animals were approaching. As one of the girls peeked in at him, Timothy slammed the door shut. He held the knob as the building shuddered and then settled into silence.

Even though he was terrified to open the door, the absolute darkness inside the small space soon became unbearable. Slowly, with his good hand, he turned the knob. A slice of light appeared. The hallway was empty. Abigail's voice rang in his memory: *They'll kill you . . . because* I'm terrified *that they will.* Could these horrors actually kill, or were the cursed only in danger from themselves, like Stuart, who'd inhaled the pool water? Timothy realized that the Nightmarys had never touched him. Sure, his hand hurt, but that was because he'd actually hit the window. That part had been real; he knew the Nightmarys were not.

Abigail had been wrong; they *could* beat these things, if they could beat their fear.

Through the railing, Timothy glanced into the foyer below. Something slammed the front door, and he froze. After a few seconds of silence, he knew he was alone. He pulled the closet door open and rushed onto the landing. He raced down the stairs. Bursting onto the front porch, he glanced down the street. Except for the waning daylight, everything looked as it had when they'd first arrived. Totally normal.

Abigail was gone, just like the old man had predicted. But how had she disappeared?

She hadn't, Timothy reasoned. Abigail had been inside the mob of girls. The Nightmarys must have surrounded her and ushered her down the stairs right past him. They weren't *coming* for him; they were *leaving* with her. But to where?

The place where your end will come, the old man had said.

The temple of the Chaos Tribe. Timothy finally understood. Jack had meant for Abigail to be the next Delia! The battery. The soul-charge for the incomplete corpse of the Daughter of Chaos.

39.

By the time Timothy reached the next corner, he felt faint. His hand hurt when he swung his arm. But he had to find Abigail. The thought of what might be happening to her at that moment nearly drove him mad.

Sure, he could ask a neighbor to call the police, but he felt that would only waste time. Besides, how could he possibly explain everything that was happening without someone locking him in a straitjacket?

Down the hill, he ran faster than ever toward his house. By the time he reached his front yard, he had to stop and catch his breath. Seconds later, something down the street captured his attention. Near the mouth of the Dragon Stairs on Edgehill Road, a girl stood perfectly still. However, as Timothy squinted into the fading daylight, the figure briefly blurred, like smudged pencil, before solidifying again.

With his lungs on fire, Timothy slowly crossed in front of his house to get a better view. When the girl waved, taunting him, strands of cobweb dangled from her arm. She disappeared down the Dragon Stairs. As he struggled to run after her, he realized she might be leading him away from where he needed to be. But if the Nightmarys traveled in a pack, maybe this single phantom would lead him to the rest of the group . . . and Abigail.

Crossing Edgehill Road, he called Abigail's name again. No answer. As he quickly approached the Dragon Stairs, he realized that the painting of the Chinese dragon, whose swirling eyes usually greeted him at this point in the road, was gone. Someone had whitewashed the staircase's wooden walls. But the painting had been there when he'd followed Abigail up the hill from the campus.

Timothy cautiously crossed the sidewalk and peered into the mouth of the tunnel. As far as he could see, until the stairwell's first zigzag turn, the walls were bare, as if the graffiti had never existed. He touched the white wall. It was dry.

The girl had led him here. Why? He turned around, glancing up the street toward his house. Was Abigail somewhere back up the hill?

In the woods, on the other side of the wall, a tree branch snapped. When it hit the ground with a loud thud, Timothy jumped. Then he froze. He suddenly had a terrible feeling that he knew what had happened to the Chinese dragon painting. And worse, he realized why the phantom girl had lured him here.

With a lump in his throat, Timothy stepped away from the mouth of the tunnel. Peering around the wall into the woods, he saw something large and green slip behind a curve in the staircase. He took a slow, deep breath.

This can't really be happening, he thought. This must be a dream—a nightmare like the one he'd had earlier that week when Ben had crawled out of the giant jar in his closet. In real life, old men did not place curses on children. In real life, groups of ghostly girls didn't kidnap his friends. In real life, paintings of enormous monsters didn't crawl off their canvases to hunt him.

Quietly, Timothy stepped backward into the street. The forest grew dark, shadows looming as the sun finally settled past the horizon across the river. He looked for any sign of movement between the trees, but the woods were still. Yet Timothy sensed a presence watching him, waiting for him to turn his back. The hill beyond the sidewalk was steep, a good hiding place for something as large as what Timothy feared might be there.

This isn't real, he thought. I'm not scared.

If he could make himself believe this, then it would be true. That was how the curse worked, wasn't it? That was the key.

Bracing himself, Timothy turned around. "I'm just walking

home," he whispered. "This is an ordinary day. I'm not scared." He crossed Edgehill Road, making his way slowly back up Beech Nut Street toward his house. "Everything is totally fine." But your hand is throbbing. Your knees ache. Abigail is gone. Doesn't that mean everything is not fine? Doesn't that mean everything that's happening . . . is *real*?

Shut up! Timothy thought at the voice in his head. He was nearly home now. His front yard stretched before him, and beyond that was his front door. Then what?

He'd call Zilpha. She'd be livid, he knew, but she was the only one who understood what was going on here; besides, any worry he had of getting yelled at was outweighed by Abigail's disappearance. He couldn't imagine her fear.

Behind him, an enormous crash shook the ground, as if one of the great oaks clinging to Edgehill's hill had tumbled down the cliff toward the college athletic fields. Timothy stopped at the bottom of the front steps and squeezed his eyes shut. Down the block, something growled—a lower rumble than any car coming up Edgehill Road with a bad exhaust pipe could possibly make. Slowly, Timothy turned around.

Crouching on the shattered remains of the Dragon Stairs tunnel was an enormous green snakelike monster, its long body twisting down the hill past the battered guardrail. Its wide black eyes spiraled and spun, trying to hypnotize Timothy, daring him to look away. It tapped its silver claws on the sidewalk and began to grin, revealing huge, sharp white teeth. Two thick orange whiskers swirled and twirled from its curled top lip, like in the painting from which they'd come. The creature's long red tongue flicked from its mouth, stretching halfway across the road. The creature didn't look angry or hungry. Its expression was more frightening than that—it reminded Timothy of a cat looking to play with its dinner.

"Delicious," it whispered in a breezy gasp of breath.

Timothy would be the mouse.

It stepped forward, dragging its long body up over the cliff, onto the street. It must have been two hundred feet long, with at least half as many *actual* feet.

Mesmerized, Timothy couldn't move. As he'd come up the street away from Edgehill Road, he had tried to force the image of the dragon becoming real out of his imagination. In a way, it had worked. This *wasn't* a real dragon, but the painting itself. The creature was flat, two-dimensional, as if it had simply peeled off the wall.

For a brief moment, Timothy's fear floated away. A *painting* could not hurt him. Then the image of the crushed stairway behind the dragon brought him back to reality . . . or at least back to whatever was pretending to be reality.

They'll kill you . . . because I'm terrified *that they will.*

Not true, Timothy hoped. What if I just close my eyes and wait for the fear to pass? Can I risk taking such a dangerous chance?

As the dragon slinked farther up the hill, it opened its mouth and bleated a high-pitched burst of laughter. It rattled the windows of his house and knocked Timothy off his feet. Falling back, he caught his ankle on the bottom step, and he hit the stairs.

Across the street, Mrs. Mendelson stood at her mailbox, collecting her mail. She glanced up at Timothy and waved. "You all right?" she called, concerned. "That was quite a tumble." Could she not see the creature approaching swiftly up the hill across her neighbors' lawns? Of course not, Timothy thought, flipping over and crawling up the steps. Lucky woman. *She* hadn't been cursed by an evil lunatic with a magical jawbone.

It's not real! Timothy screamed inside his head, trying desperately to assure himself that if he glanced over his shoulder, the Dragon Stairs would be intact, and the only thing racing across the damp lawns of Beech Nut Street would be a cool evening breeze. As he ran across the porch for the front door, he tried to come up with an *actual* solution to defeat the monster if his brain wouldn't let him *think* his way out of it. Before he grappled with the front doorknob, another screeching roar shook him, rustling his hair, his clothes, his bones. Timothy couldn't help but turn around.

The dragon had made its way to Timothy's house, tapping hundreds of silver claws, the foremost of which were now inching slowly up the base of the driveway. Its black eyes spun, trying to capture his attention.

Timothy had an idea. He called to Mrs. Mendelson, who was now crossing her lawn carrying a small pile of mail, "Nice day, don't you think?"

His neighbor stopped and turned around, surprised. "Oh, it was lovely," she said. "I hope you were able to spend some time outside after the awful weather we had this week."

The dragon paused a few feet up the driveway, confused by their conversation. The rest of its cartoonlike body wriggled all the way down the block. At the stop sign, its sharp green tail flicked. The dragon was angry at being interrupted.

"Yeah, actually," said Timothy, trying to steady his voice, his heart still thumping so hard in his chest that it hurt, "I got to do some *serious* running around." He leaned against the doorknob, trying with his good hand to turn it. But it was locked. He pressed the doorbell. Inside, the chimes rang, but that was all. His dad wasn't home. Timothy had left his bag behind and didn't have his key.

"Well, good for you," said Mrs. Mendelson. "I wish I still had the energy for running around. This is the most exercise I've gotten all week." She waved the mail above her head, turned around, and continued across her front yard. "Good night, Timothy," she called over her shoulder.

The dragon seemed to smile, lowering its head, resuming its ascent up his driveway.

"Wait!" Timothy answered. The old woman paused. "Mrs. Mendelson, do you have a key to my house? I accidentally locked myself out."

"Hmm," she said, "that's a good question." She stared at the sky, racking her brain for an answer. "I know I have some neighborhood keys, but I don't think your parents ever gave—"

The dragon was too close now for Timothy to wait for her response. Its claws click-clacked their way farther up the pavement, halfway to the house's front walk. Its scales glistened with painted violet highlights. Puffs of white cartoonish smoke—outlined with thick black graffiti strokes—wafted from its flared nostrils.

Timothy noticed a dirt-filled plaster pot that his mother had recently placed on the front porch, with the intention of filling it with pansies. The planter was heavy, and his injured hand begged him to stop, but he managed to lift it, then shuffled toward the bay window in his mother's piano room. With a great heave, Timothy tossed the pot through the window, shattering the glass onto the Victorian love seat just inside. Ignoring Mrs. Mendelson's shriek, Timothy leapt through the opening, tearing his jeans on the jagged bottom edge. He tumbled onto the floor next to the planter. Without looking back, he jumped up and barreled into the foyer, where the phone sat on the side table. He snatched it from its cradle and reached into his pocket for the scrap of envelope with Zilpha's phone number on it.

His hands shook as he tried to dial her number. Timothy noticed a splash of green dash around the side of the house. He spun, trying to keep it in sight, but it quickly disappeared. "Pick up, pick up, pick up," he whispered as the phone rang. Then the line went dead. Timothy fell against the nearest wall.

Something hit the back of the house. Every piece of furniture shifted two inches closer to the front door. Timothy screamed. He dropped the phone and crept toward the kitchen. Through the window above the table, one great, spiraling eye watched him. Timothy screamed again. That horrible, laughing screech roared through the walls. Then a booming voice said, "I'm going to eat you, little boy."

Thinking quickly of the game he used to play with Stuart, Timothy shouted, "But . . . I'm filled with slime. Totally disgusting. You'd hate me!"

Wide-eyed, the dragon screeched again. "Then I will only *stomp* you." The house shook again as the dragon slammed itself against the wall, cracking the plaster and shattering glass past the stove. Timothy clutched the doorframe. As the green monster's face reeled away from the window, cartoon smoke billowed from its nostrils.

Timothy realized what was coming next but didn't know what to do. Run upstairs? Hide in the basement? No, he had to get far away from here. Even if he was the only one in his neighborhood who could see this creature, he was afraid that wouldn't stop the curse.

Through the window, the dragon flared its nostrils and opened its mouth. Then, like a giant disgusting sneeze, red paint streamed forth from its nose. Timothy ducked into the hallway. The paint splashed past him toward the front door.

Seconds later, the red paint became animated licks of flame, coloring the floor, walls, and furniture with graffiti fire.

It's like a cartoon, thought Timothy. Harmless.

When he noticed the wallpaper beginning to bubble, turn
brown, and peel away from the plaster, he changed his mind. The hallway in which he stood was growing hot. He had no idea how to put out a cartoon fire that was well on its way to burning down his house. Timothy peered around the edge of the door. To his horror, there was a giant hole in the kitchen wall, rimmed by red flickering licks of graffiti paint. Flat white smoke was beginning to fill the small room. The dragon was nowhere to be seen.

Covering his mouth with his sleeve, Timothy dashed around the corner into the kitchen and leapt over the growing flames. He barreled out the back door and down the steps. The bushes against the house had also been splattered with paint and were burning. He ran into his backyard away from the flames, glancing around for a sign of another attack.

He heard a creaking sound above him. Looking up, he found the dragon smiling down from the house's roof. "I have changed my mind," said the dragon. "I will not stomp you. Instead, I will roast you." A burst of painted fire bloomed as it shot from the dragon's mouth. Timothy swiveled and dashed toward the garage, avoiding the splatter of red, which quickly began to smolder and spread, blackening the grass beneath it.

Without hesitation, Timothy careened through the garage's side door, pulling it shut behind him. Leaning against the door, he had a terrible realization. From where the dragon sat on the house, it had a perfect shot at this building. There had to be a way to stop this.

Looking around, he noticed his father's golf clubs sitting in the far corner, but those wouldn't help. The dinged-up red lawn mower was propped against the far wall. Mow him down? thought Timothy. I don't think so.

Something on a shelf above the mower caught Timothy's attention: a small tin of turpentine. Paint thinner.

The ground rocked as the dragon's long body poured from the roof into the yard. Through the side door's small window, Timothy saw a sea of swirling green serpent, roiling and rolling like ocean waves.

Timothy made for the shelves, sliding on his rear end over the hood of his mother's car. He reached for the canister, but his fingers grazed it, and it clattered to the ground. When he picked up the tin, his heart sank; only a small bit of liquid sloshed around at the bottom.

"Where did you go, little boy?" said the dragon. "You cannot hide from me."

He didn't see me come in here! thought Timothy. At least I have time to—

The huge pinwheel of an eye appeared at the small window. Timothy screamed and tripped over the lawn mower.

"Aha!" chortled the dragon. "Now you die."

Timothy clutched the nearly empty canister. Scrambling around his mother's car, he ran toward the side door. In seconds, the garage would be engulfed in red graffiti flame. Would Timothy burn? He kicked the side door open, so hard it banged against the outside wall. Timothy flicked open the turpentine tin's cap and held it up toward the dragon's amused face.

"No," Timothy shouted. "I don't!" Then he squeezed.

A thin spray shot from the nozzle. The liquid was not much, but Timothy managed to shoot it directly into the monster's wild eyes. For a few seconds, the creature blinked, as if in shock, then began to wail. It twisted its body into tight coils, writhing in pain. When it opened its eyes again, the black-and-white spirals, which had moments earlier been spinning like a hypnotist's trick, were melting in tears down the creature's green face.

"I cannot see," cried the dragon. "You are a powerful sorcerer."

"Damn straight," said Timothy. "I'm a powerful . . ." He immediately regretted saying anything, because the dragon followed his voice and spit buckets of flame in his direction. Timothy spun into the garage again, just missing being drenched in red paint, which hit the clapboard instead. He watched as the garage's wall went up in flickering curls of red.

He had an idea. He ran around to the driver's door of his mother's car. He opened it and hopped in. The key was still in the ignition from the night before, when he'd moved the car

for his father. He turned the key, and the engine sparked to life. Timothy grappled with the gearshift, flipping it into reverse the way his father had often showed him.

Outside, the dragon flailed, knocking itself against what remained of the house. The sound of splintering wood rang out into the early evening. Screaming in pain, the creature wrapped its tail around the oak tree that separated Timothy's and Stuart's yards, then began to pound its weight against the ground in waves.

It felt as though an earthquake was rattling the hill. Timothy was so shaken he could barely keep his foot aligned with the gas pedal. Still, he managed to slam it to the floor. The tires squealed, and the car shot backward, crashing into the garage door. To Timothy's surprise, the large wooden door broke away from the frame in several large pieces. Timothy forced the car over the rubble and out of the burning building. His father would have a fit when he came home and saw this mess.

At the sound of the car squealing into the driveway, the

dragon's head rose high above the yard. Its blind eyes were useless, but it could hear fine. It jolted forward across the small path between the garage and the house. Timothy didn't wait for the creature to find him—he gunned the gas and flew down the driveway into the street. Swinging the wheel to the right, he pointed the front of the car down the hill. Then he shifted into drive. He pulled away from the spot so quickly he left black marks on the pavement.

When Timothy glanced in the rearview mirror, the smoldering, ruined house shrank with the distance. He quickly approached the intersection at Edgehill Road. The smashed staircase was directly in front of him. If he didn't brake soon, he'd simply fly over the cliff. Somehow, his foot found its way to the other pedal, and he managed to pause for a moment at the stop sign. With another quick glance up the hill, he saw the creature slithering blindly into the middle of the road, its mouth open wide in frustration, its whiskers whipping wildly.

If he hadn't almost peed in his pants, he would have thought that was pretty cool.

40.

Timothy drove quickly, steadily. He kept close to the guardrail. His brain was so fried, he couldn't remember which turn led to his father's garage, so he went south on Edgehill Road toward the college's main campus and the Taft Bridge, wiping tears and snot from his upper lip.

It was getting quite dark out now, so he flipped on the headlights. Finally, the wooded slope on the right was replaced by several small houses. Then Timothy saw the tall, dark silhouette of a building rising beyond the bridge entrance, across from the campus's main gate—the Mayfair.

At the bridge intersection, Timothy drove through a stoplight. A few cars honked their horns, and he was shocked back to reality. Now that he was surrounded by traffic, he was terrified that he might smash into someone or something. He took his foot off the gas, and as the hill began to slope upward, the car slowed. More vehicles coming off the bridge honked their horns. Timothy pressed his foot down, and the car jerked forward.

"Come on," he said. "Only a little farther."

Steadying the wheel, Timothy drove up the center of Shutter Avenue, staying clear of the cars parked on either side of the road. The Mayfair was on his right.

The street was full. No room for parking. Timothy simply stopped next to a small red sports car, shoved the gearshift into park, and turned off the engine. He grabbed the keys from the ignition. When he opened the driver's door, a speeding truck wailed its horn as it drove by. Timothy waved an apology and climbed out of the car. Shaking, he stared up at the tall building, then crossed the sidewalk into the main garden.

Ahead, the spidery iron door swung open. Inside stood the uniformed man Timothy had met earlier that week. The man smiled, but as Timothy limped closer, the man's expression changed. "You okay, little dude?"

"I—I need to see Mrs. Kindred."

"Sure," said the doorman. "Just let me give her a call." He headed toward his desk, but Timothy didn't wait. He crossed through the large empty lobby toward the elevator bank. "Hey, hold up, kid," said the doorman. But Timothy had already hit the button. The elevator door immediately opened, so he slipped inside.

As the car took him swiftly upward, he worried that Jack might be visiting Zilpha's neighbor, Georgia. Or maybe he had returned for Zilpha herself? Timothy wondered what he'd do if he found an open door, an empty apartment, signs of struggle, or worse. . . .

Moments later, at the top floor, Timothy had to force himself to step out into the small hallway. To his relief, there was no graffiti, cobwebs, or creepy little girls waiting for him. He crossed quickly to the big black door marked 16B.

Timothy knocked, quietly at first, then harder as he waited. He began to worry that no one was home. Then deep inside the apartment, he heard the sound of barking. Long fingernails clicked against the wood floor. The little dog, Hepzibah, skittered toward him. She sniffed at the bottom of the door. Finally, the old woman's voice, shaking and tired, said, "Who's here, Hep?"

"It's me," Timothy cried. "I need your help!"

The old woman opened the door, her brow crinkled. She wore the same purple kimono he'd seen her in from the octagonal window on Ash Tree Lane, now with a green silk scarf tied around her head. "Come in," she said immediately. "Mario said someone was coming up. But I didn't expect . . ." She shook her head in disbelief. "What happened to you?"

Timothy slinked through the doorway, trying not to collapse. "Abigail's gone. Jack . . . Johnson Harwood took her. He has the jawbone. He's cursed me and her, and probably you too. He's planning on using Abigail to charge the . . . corpse. We need to find her before it's too late."

Zilpha closed the door behind her. "Calm down, Timothy," she said forcefully. She led him into the dining room and pulled out a chair. "Sit. Breathe." She stared at him for a moment. "Johnson Harwood did what? Abigail is where?"

Timothy sat next to her and tried his best to recount everything that had happened. The book he'd found. The office in the library. The baseball cards. The house on Ash Tree Lane. Mr. Harwood's confession. The Nightmarys. And finally, the dragon.

Zilpha was stunned. For several seconds after Timothy finished his story, she opened and closed her mouth like a fish out of water, struggling to breathe. "Abigail's not in New Jersey?"

Timothy turned emergency-red as he admitted his betrayal. "I spent the entire day with her. We were locked in the attic together when you came to Jack's house. We shouted and shouted, but Georgia thought it was his television."

For a long time, Zilpha held her hand to her mouth, staring at the table. Her eyes flicked back and forth slightly. "I should have known better," she said finally. She closed her eyes and took a deep breath. "I thought I had settled everything when I destroyed Harwood's trinket this afternoon. Stupid. I should have realized who I was dealing with this morning when Georgia told me he'd been here at the Mayfair.

That he was her boyfriend! Quite a significant coincidence, don't you think? And I ignored the biggest clue!" She pounded the table with her palms. "He *knew* I was coming," Zilpha continued, "and he was prepared. He tricked me. I destroyed the wrong artifact." She took Timothy's hand, staring into his eyes. "Abigail is in serious trouble. She is somewhere in New Starkham. We need to figure out where."

"But how?" said Timothy.

"You've solved plenty of clues so far. I trust there may be some left to uncover?"

"I can't think of any."

Zilpha pointed at the desk in the corner of the room. "Grab a pencil and paper. I always find it helpful to make a list." A few minutes later, Timothy had written out several lists summarizing everything he thought he knew and everything he was unsure of, everything he'd been through and everything he feared was coming.

Zilpha eyed the list and shook her head. "Can you think of anything else to narrow all this down? Anything at all?"

From outside, the familiar old foghorn called a lonely cry over the river. The sound struck Timothy as odd. The weather had been clear all day.

Timothy glanced over his shoulder toward the French doors. Though the sky was now dark, Timothy watched as strange clouds obscured a bright moon coming over the horizon. He rose from his chair and went to the window.

From all directions, the weather seemed to be gathering, like a hurricane eye, drawing an ominous target around New Starkham. "Something's happening," said Timothy. "Look."

Zilpha joined him at the window. "At what?"

"The clouds. I've seen them before, in a painting at the museum this week." The foghorn cried again.

"I don't see any clouds," said Zilpha.

Timothy shivered. This must be the curse, coming for him again. *"The Edge of Doom,"* he said.

"The edge of what?"

"That's the name of the painting. It's the jawbone. I'm seeing things." Timothy remembered the image: the pit of fire, the glowing sky.

"For the past few months, whenever I saw something scary," said Zilpha, "I tried to figure out some way to get around it. When the ceramic monkey my husband gave me on our fortieth anniversary snarled at me, I smashed him on the floor, then swept up the pieces. That's how I've survived these past months—little tricks. How did you get away from the dragon?"

"Turpentine," said Timothy. "I washed out his eyes."

"Brilliant!" said Zilpha, grabbing his good hand. "You've got to find something like that to combat what you're seeing now."

"But what's coming is really bad," said Timothy, shaking his head. "Whatever it is, it's going to be much bigger than the graffiti dragon. Jack is trying to stop us. We're running out of time."

"That's what he thinks," said the old woman, twisting the tail of her head wrap around her wrist. "He's forgotten who he's dealing with here. He hasn't stopped me yet."

Timothy opened the door and stepped onto the roof deck. "Can I?" he asked Zilpha. She answered by following him. The clouds were getting darker, edging closer, surrounding the city, covering what now appeared to be a full moon. The foghorn cried again. Timothy crossed to the far railing so he could see the river, the bridge, and beyond that, Rhode Island. Something flashed at the river's edge. The lighthouse was up and running.

Then it hit him: *A light in the darkness.*

In Hesselius's abandoned office, those words had been written on the mat of the lighthouse photo on the wall. His brother's motto. *This* was his order amidst the chaos. In the photo, the lighthouse had been called Hesselius's Illuminarium. The professor had even designed it. According to the articles Abigail had shown him at the library, the cults had built their temples at the convergence of great chaos. Crossroads. Mountains.

Rivers?

"I know where she is!" said Timothy.

* * *

In the elevator, halfway to the ground floor, Zilpha became flustered. "How are we getting there? I don't think a taxi will drop us off on the edge of a cliff. I wish Georgia didn't hate me right now, or I'd ask her."

"I've got a car," Timothy blurted.

"Oh, yes," said Zilpha. "You *did* mention that, didn't you?"

The elevator stopped, the doors slid open. Timothy crossed slowly through the lobby with Zilpha. Mario opened the front door. "Good night, Mrs. Kindred," he said with a worried look.

"Thank you, Mario," she answered with an emphatic smile. "Good night." In the garden, she changed her tone. "I don't know about this, Timothy. You shouldn't be driving at your age, and at my age, my eyes aren't very good. We cancel each other out."

"My dad owns a garage," he said. "And I made it here by myself. We can make it a little farther together, don't you think?"

41.

Zilpha fussed in her seat as Timothy turned left at the stop sign. He headed toward the bridge. More and more, the atmosphere resembled the painting at the museum. The black clouds now filled the entire sky, spiraling slowly like a whirlpool. Zilpha still didn't seem to notice. Timothy thought about what she'd said: little tricks would end the fear. But what trick might stop *clouds* from swirling?

"Watch out!" cried Zilpha as Timothy came up too quickly at the stoplight. The traffic whizzed past in both directions.

"Sorry," said Timothy. "I'm not used to this."

"I didn't mean to snap," she apologized. "You're . . . doing very well." The light turned green, and Timothy jerked the car forward into the intersection. Out of the corner of his eye, he noticed Zilpha tightening her seat belt.

Soon they were traveling alongside other cars, heading

west across the river. Timothy maintained his speed, even as his heart raced.

At the edge of the bridge, Timothy turned the wheel sharply, forcing his mother's car off the highway onto a small service road. Gravel spun out from under his tires, and Zilpha held tightly on to the door handle. Straining to see better, Timothy leaned forward across the steering wheel. The service road followed the edge of the cliff for several hundred yards before ending abruptly at a guardrail.

A bright light flashed over the side of the cliff. The lighthouse. Timothy noticed a staircase entrance next to the guardrail. He and Zilpha both slipped outside. Timothy helped the old woman across the rocky path.

Finally, they came to a barrier fence and a cliffside sign that read, LITTLE HUSKETOMIC LIGHTHOUSE. "In the photo, it was called Hesselius's Illuminarium," said Timothy. "Is this the same lighthouse?"

"They must have taken Hesselius's name off it after everything that happened," said Zilpha, holding on to the nearby railing. "A long time ago, people wanted to forget."

Leaning over the precipice, Timothy peered at the first step. The staircase descended steeply along the cliff face. Unlike the Dragon Stairs, these steps hugged the bluff in a straight drop, stopping at a wide outcropping that stretched out fifty feet below. From the stairs' base, a narrow path led to the lighthouse itself—a small white cone of a building, surrounded by squat shrubbery, a glass cage perched at the top, inside which rotated a blinding, iridescent light.

"Abigail's down there somewhere," said Timothy, staring at the dark stairs. The river splashed at the rocks below. He quickly returned to the car; he knew he'd find a couple of flashlights in the trunk. He handed one to Zilpha and kept one for himself. "We've got to hurry," he said, rushing back to the stairs. He took the first few steps, but turned around when he realized Zilpha was not following him.

"Go ahead," she said, worried. "I'd only hold you up. If I rush and fall, you'll have to help me as well as Abigail. Right now, she's what matters." Zilpha looked down at him, her face illuminated by another bright, brief turn from the lighthouse. Her brown eyes were liquid. "Please . . . *please* be careful. I'll be right behind you, coming at my own pace. If you need anything . . . scream."

Those were not reassuring words, but he nodded and turned around. Nauseated, he took one more step down the precipice. The dark clouds over the city seemed to change. A dim yellow light appeared in the sky. A hollow rushing sound echoed off the rock.

Timothy realized he was standing on the actual Edge of Doom. The curse. Dammit. He grasped the wooden railing that was bolted to the rock, trying to steady himself. Something strange was happening to the river. The water, which had been rushing and lapping the shore in white waves, receded, leaving the black rocks to glisten, reflecting the bridge lights from above. The river was sinking, disappearing into a deep abyss that now separated the two shores. A dark chasm had formed beyond the drop at the left of the stairs. Slowly, as if from deep within the earth, another light appeared. Lava, magma, or possibly something living and nameless, began to rise, shaking the ground with the speed of its approach.

Timothy shoved his body against the cliff, the railing pressing into his lower spine. He repeated the sentence, "This isn't happening," over and over, until finally, he heard Zilpha's voice calling to him from several steps up.

"Timothy? What's wrong?"

"The curse . . . I can't."

"Fight it," she demanded. "Fight it like you fought the dragon."

How? If this is the Edge of Doom . . . ? Timothy thought back to the day at the museum when he'd imitated the voice of the robed man on the cliff, when Abigail had thought he was making fun of her. The man in the painting had been chanting a spell or a prayer or something. Maybe Timothy could do the same. He tried to find his voice. "I . . . Timothy July . . . master of this . . . domain . . . do beseech thee . . . to leave this place . . . and return to . . . wherever the heck you came from." The ground began to shake. Mammoth red, scaly hands reached up out of the chasm, claws the size of cars grasping at the space just below the Taft Bridge. Fighting back a scream, Timothy clutched at the railing and closed his eyes. Then, angry, he cried as loudly as he could, *"IN THE NAME OF CHAOS, GO THE HELL AWAY!"*

Everything went still. Timothy listened to his heart beating in his eardrums. When he opened his eyes, the sky had cleared. The red light was gone. And most important, the claws had disappeared. The water splashed against the rocks, and the stars glittered in the sky. There was no Edge of Doom. This was only the edge of the Little Husketomic.

But then he noticed the bright light of the full moon higher up in the sky. This was no illusion. He was running out of time.

"It—it worked," Timothy stammered, glancing over his shoulder at Zilpha. "I'll be right back."

Timothy rushed down the endless stairs, holding on to the railing with his good hand, trying not to slip on the slick boards. He leapt the last two steps onto a gravel path. The sound of the river was deafening, but it was a comfort to hear, as opposed to the horrible rushing sound of the thing that had, moments earlier, been rising from the chasm. As Timothy ran, every few seconds, the path was lit by the light from above, so he was able to quickly follow it to the small clapboard building.

Standing in front of a shiny black metal door, Timothy caught his breath. Glancing back up the cliff, he saw Zilpha sitting on a stair near the top, inching her way slowly down.

42.

Timothy expected the door to be locked, but to his surprise, the knob turned in his hand. He released it, and the door slowly opened a crack. Timothy stared into the musty darkness. From inside the building, a grinding sound grumbled, the whirring of an ancient engine, the light turning on its old axle.

He kicked the door and it swung open. The whirring sound was louder now. Timothy almost called out *Hello?* but imagined Jack hiding somewhere inside. He peered into the dark room and soon realized that it was not as dark as it had first seemed.

The room was a perfect circle. Bolted to the wall, a rickety metal staircase swirled around the circumference of the building, ending at an open hatch in the ceiling twenty feet up. From the hatch, every fifteen seconds, the bright light burst forth, but the rest of the time, a dull phosphorescence spilled into the room, dusting the furniture and equipment with a ghostly glow.

Timothy looked around. The room reminded him of Hesselius's abandoned office—filled with antiques, maps, photos of the surrounding landscape—except that someone had obviously recently been here, possibly even worked here on a regular basis. There was a stack of papers on a nearby desk. A computer. A telephone. A tall halogen floor lamp. A modern-looking office chair. Timothy quickly realized he'd seen all there was to see.

Maybe Abigail was upstairs? The rusting bolts attached to the walls told him it might not be a safe climb.

Timothy closed the door, so that no one might slip in behind him. Crossing to the lamp, he flicked the switch, filling the room with white light. He stood in the center of the room and spun one last time to see if he'd missed a clue, when his sneaker caught in a groove in the concrete floor. Looking down, Timothy gasped.

Familiar words were carved there: *Righteousness, Integrity, Sacrifice.* Earlier that day, he'd noticed these words stitched in a triangle on a gray flag in Hesselius's office. But here, under Timothy's feet, the words were arranged differently. Etched in the stone, the words radiated from a single point, like a three-pronged star. Surrounding the words was a halo of engraved numbers about six feet in diameter.

Timothy bent down to examine the carvings more closely. Brushing the concrete with his fingertips, he noticed that this part of the floor had been built in several fragments. The words had each been sculpted into a separate triangle of concrete, and each number surrounding the center triangle was contained within its own single stone. Timothy stood up and stepped away to get a better view. He read the words again, then traced the circle of numerals several times, trying to glean a pattern.

435, 102, 340, 921, 556, 900, 167, 761, 149, 899, 255, 929, 320, 532, 203, 230 . . .

Timothy knew he was missing something.

Then, just like that, the answer struck him.

Carlton Quigley. Bucky Jenkins. Leroy "Two Fingers" Fromm. The writing from *The Clue of the Incomplete Corpse.* The baseball cards. Christian's clue to his son. The jersey numbers had been the safe's combination. Once Jack Harwood had discovered his father's secret office and opened the safe, he'd pieced the puzzle together in the same way Timothy had. The journal inside must have pointed Harwood here, across the river.

Timothy thought of Hesselius's clue: the names in the book. Maybe this emblem was another part of it? The numbers on the floor were different than the jersey numbers. Bigger. But not too big for page numbers . . . He closed his eyes, trying to picture the names on the pages and the order Harwood had mentioned. First, second, and third base. Jenkins, Quigley, then Fromm.

Bucky Jenkins . . . Page 149? Slowly, Timothy crossed the circle and pressed his foot against the stone with the number 149 carved into it. It took a bit of effort, but the stone descended a few inches into the floor and something deep underneath the building shook and clicked into place. *Yes!* Timothy thought.

Next came Carlton Quigley.

He crossed to the stone that read 102. He pressed his sneaker against the stone, and it too sank a few inches into the floor. Another deep click rattled the building.

One more number to go. Leroy "Two Fingers" Fromm.

Timothy thought for a long time. He wasn't sure which number to step on. He imagined that each stone might be capable of sinking. He figured he could try stepping on all of the stones, and see which ones descended. But what if he stepped on a wrong number and screwed something up? Abigail had mentioned that Christian Hesselius had been interested in the engineering feats of ancient civilizations. This place might be booby-trapped. He decided he couldn't take any chances; he needed to remember the code correctly. He glanced around the circle one more time, then intuitively moved toward two adjacent stones: 203 and 230. His memory assured him it was one of these, but he wasn't quite certain which one. They were too similar. Hesselius might have arranged them to throw off an intruder like him. Timothy took a deep breath, and tried once again to imagine the book.

He saw the cover, the title, the look on Zelda Kite's face. The jacket was tattered. The pages were yellowed. Fromm had been written on a right-hand page, just like Jenkins on 149. An odd number.

Fromm must be an odd number too.

The answer was 203.

Tentatively, he stepped on that stone and felt it sink into the floor. Another solid clicking sound shook the building; then suddenly, the floor began to tremble. Timothy scuttled away from the circle, watching from a safe spot near the desk as dust puffed out from the cracks between the stones. One by one, each triangular panel slid straight down into the floor. First went *Righteousness.* Then *Integrity.* And finally, *Sacrifice.*

By the time the lighthouse had settled again into the sound of its steady engine whirring, a steep spiral staircase had descended into the floor. The numbered stones had risen, erasing the code, once more becoming level with the rest of the concrete slab. Each of the word panels had lowered to form a step, each step two feet lower than its predecessor, ending at *Sacrifice.* From there, a dark, ragged gash in the bedrock opened into a rough-hewn tunnel directly underneath the building.

Timothy held his sleeve to his mouth, marveling at the gaping black hole, until the dust had dissipated.

He flicked his flashlight on and off to be sure it still worked. By shining the beam into the new hole, Timothy revealed a steep, wet slope that disappeared at an early bend in the black passage. No way, Timothy thought. I have to go down *there*?

But he had no choice. The full moon was rising, and he had to find Abigail.

As he climbed down the spiral steps and into the tunnel, Timothy's last thought was of Zilpha edging down the stairs. He hoped she'd be okay.

In the dark, he concentrated on the tight walls and low ceiling. He forced himself to take deep breaths, as if that would help the tunnel expand. The steep floor was slick with moisture. Rocks jutted every few feet, creating makeshift stairs. Every step he took echoed into the earth. The flashlight glinted off the rock, reflecting cobwebs and several large white scurrying insects. Timothy backed away, as if the bugs might suddenly grow huge and attack him. He leapt over them quickly and kept moving forward. Every time water dripped into his face from the ceiling, Timothy yelped, wiping it quickly away. After he passed an especially tight squeeze between the rocks, he almost started to hyperventilate. How much farther? The flashlight beam shook as his hand trembled. Looking into the infinite darkness, he squeaked, "Abigail?" His voice mocked him as it mimicked him, passing up and down the tunnel like a rodent searching desperately for a way out. Timothy felt the same.

He closed his eyes and imagined his brother, not the

zombie version, but the real one, who was somewhere in Maryland, lying unconscious in a bed. His brother was a hero. Timothy thought he must try to be one too.

When he opened his eyes again, the walls had receded. The ceiling was higher. Timothy could actually stand up straight. Ahead, several grim tunnels went deeper into the earth. Even if he knew the right way, he was unsure he could bring himself to go any farther.

Accidentally sweeping the flashlight at the wall beside him, Timothy noticed a large iron door, rusted black. Swung inward nearly a foot, it revealed another dark cavern. Two L-shaped brackets were attached to the outside of the door. On the floor lay a wooden plank, longer than the width of the iron slab. When fitted into the brackets, it appeared, the plank would lock the door shut from the outside. Timothy listened to the darkness inside. Very faintly, he heard someone breathing. His own throat began to close. "Abigail?" he managed to whisper.

Moments later, he heard a high-pitched moan from inside the room.

Abigail!

Timothy threw his body against the heavy door and pushed it open even farther. The rusting hinges squealed, but the door gave way, scraping against the floor.

As he shined the light into the new cavern, the first thing Timothy noticed was a pale lump sitting in the middle of what looked like a pile of rubble. The shape glanced at him, showing a grubby face and black hair. Abigail's eyes were red-rimmed and wide with terror. Someone had bound her mouth with what looked like strands of white cobweb. With her arms behind her back, she'd been tied to a wooden column that stretched from the floor to the ceiling.

As Timothy took a step into the room, he noticed with horror that the rubble under Abigail was crumbling grayish bones. They're only bones, he told himself, feeling as though he might faint. But then Abigail made a pleading noise. "We'll get out of here," he promised. "Don't be scared."

Something was moving in one of the tunnels behind him. Timothy spun, shining the flashlight into the darkness. He screamed as a pair of cobweb-covered claws reached for his face. A Nightmary. She swooped closer, her face shifting underneath her veil. He swung the flashlight up at her, but his hand passed through the illusion and the girl disappeared. The flashlight slipped out of his hand, fell to the floor, and rolled against the far wall outside the chamber. With a shout, Timothy toppled backward into the room with Abigail.

Before he caught his balance, strong hands grabbed his shoulders and pulled him deeper into the chamber. Timothy hit the ground as someone rushed past him and out the door. He quickly turned and glanced at the entry. The beam from his flashlight moved as someone picked it up. Timothy tried to crawl back toward the metal slab. Before he could reach out and grab hold of it, he saw a face peek at him from around the edge.

Jack grinned and said, "Good night, children." Then the old man yanked the door shut.

43.

Timothy blindly examined the door, searching for a handle, but there was none. He shouted, "Let us out!", then quickly realized how silly he was being. This chamber was no illusion, and the little tricks he'd been using to beat the curse were useless now. Chanting a spell wouldn't work so well this time.

Oh my God, oh my God, oh my God.

What would his family think when he never came home? What would they tell Ben when he finally woke up? What would happen to Zilpha on the stairs? Would Jack—Johnson Harwood—find her on his way back up? He wanted to curl into a ball and go to sleep. *Dreamless* sleep.

Behind him, Abigail began to emit a garbled sound from behind her gag, and that brought him back to reality. "Ack—Ahh—Ket," she said. He followed her voice in the darkness and nearly tripped over her.

"Oh my gosh, Abigail, are you okay?" He reached out and touched her shoulder. Her arms were yanked backward and her wrists were bound around the wooden pole. "Here, I'll untie you." He managed to pull the gag away from her mouth, but the rope around her wrists was stringy and tight. He couldn't even tell where to begin.

"Back pocket," Abigail croaked.

"What have you got . . . ?" Then he remembered. Her lighter. The one she'd stolen from her father in New Jersey.

A Light in the Darkness. Of course.

He felt a small square lump tucked snugly into Abigail's jeans. He reached into her pocket with the index finger of his good hand and scooped the lighter up and out. It clattered to the ground. He blindly sorted through the pile of rubble, pushing the thought of old bones out of his head. He located a warm metallic object and picked it up. "I found it," he said. "What do I do? If I light it, I'll burn you!"

"Try," said Abigail, her voice wavering desperately.

"Okay." He flipped the lighter's lid open. Positioning it under Abigail's wrists, he said, "Pull your arms as far apart as possible." Then he pressed the flint switch.

A yellow spark lit up the darkness, then went out. From where Timothy sat, in that brief moment, he thought he saw a tall, thin figure standing in the corner of the chamber. A lump formed in his throat. He didn't mention the sight to Abigail. He simply tried the flint again. It was harder now since his hands were shaking. Another spark, longer this time. Another glimpse of the figure. Now it was closer, maybe fifteen feet away. Timothy was certain he could hear the shuffling of skin against the wet stone.

"Hurry," said Abigail.

Trembling, Timothy flicked the lighter again. This time, the flame caught hold, and shadows danced all around the

room. Now the figure was closer, and Timothy could see it clearly. Its dirty white hair fell across its skeletal face, past its wide shoulders. Sinewy muscle clung to its jutting bones. Ragged robes, mere black tatters, draped the creature's torso. It seemed to wobble as it shuffled closer to the wooden column. It held its arms toward them, its long fingers tensed, as if anticipating a large meal. *Is that Delia?* he thought. Abigail groaned. Timothy didn't know whether she noticed the creature or if the flame was biting her skin. *Just a few seconds longer . . .*

The creature continued forward, bringing a horrible stench with it. Finally, Timothy could see its face. Its eye sockets were empty, and its mouth was already open. In its bottom jaw glinted a single sharp black tooth.

No, Timothy now knew, *that's not Delia. I'm crouching on what's left of Delia. Full moon's outside. That thing is the Daughter of Chaos. . . .*

The cobweb cords snapped, and Abigail leapt to her feet. Timothy dropped the lighter. The room was again pitched into darkness. He imagined the creature slowly closing the distance. He stood up, reaching for Abigail's arm. She hugged him tightly, then whispered, "Where's the lighter?"

"I don't know," he said. "It fell somewhere over here."

Together, they bent down, sweeping the ground near the column. "Got it," said Abigail, seconds later. Timothy heard the top flip open, then saw a spark as Abigail once again lit the flame.

"Watch out!" he cried.

The creature was directly behind Abigail, outstretched fingers nearly at her neck. He pulled her away, around the other side of the wooden column. The flame disappeared again. When he took Abigail's hand, he felt the closed lighter in her palm. Together, they lurched toward the large iron door.

Abigail whispered, sounding frantic. "I remember being surrounded by the Nightmarys. Next thing I knew, I was tied to that column. Mr. Harwood was shining a flashlight into a darker corner of the room. Whatever bone Gramma crushed was a fake. He took the real jawbone out of his pocket, whispered something, and plugged it into that thing's skull. I was so scared. . . ." Her voice wavered. "I tried to do what you said, handle my fear. But it didn't work, Timothy."

"That's because you were really tied there," he answered. "It wasn't part of the curse."

"Then you showed up," she continued. "I saw one of the Nightmarys come up behind you, and when you swung, your hand went right through it."

"Right," said Timothy. "An illusion."

"An illusion," Abigail echoed, as the idea seemed to sink in. From the darkness came a hushed exhalation, like a gasp through a crushed voice box. "*That* was not an illusion."

The corpse was growing frustrated. Timothy and Abigail immediately turned to the cold metal slab, but without a handle to pull, they were trapped.

Timothy heard Abigail flip the lighter top open again. "Wait," he whispered.

"Why?"

"It'll sense us. Don't light it yet." They listened for a moment. The creature sounded like it was near the wooden column. "In the darkness, maybe it goes directly to the pole where we were tied. Like a habit?"

"Or what if it can see in the dark?" said Abigail. "What if it's heading for us right now?"

Timothy pressed himself against the iron door. "I—I have an idea," he said.

"Does it involve drop-kicking this skinny beast?" said Abigail. "Because if so, I'm totally up for it."

"Not quite," said Timothy. "But I'm thinking, if this corpse's power comes from the tooth, maybe we should try to take the jawbone."

"What do you mean . . . take?"

"I mean, if Harwood stuck the jawbone into its mouth

and activated it, then maybe if we reach in, pull it back out, that would deactivate it?"

Abigail laughed. "You want to reach into its mouth? Are you crazy? How do we get close enough to do that?"

"Getting close won't be the hard part."

"And what if it doesn't work, Timothy? What if it grabs us and . . . does whatever it does, before we get a chance to—?"

"I don't know!" said Timothy. "But can you think of another option?"

Abigail was silent. A few seconds later, she said, "Okay."

"Okay?"

"You're right. If we're trapped in here, we're going to die either way. And I'd rather keep my soul, thank you very much. I'll light the flame. You do the jaw snatching. Deal?"

Timothy gulped. "Deal."

Abigail pressed the flint button, the spark burst, and the flame flickered from her fingertips. The creature crouched near the column, scratching at the wood. At the sight of the fire, it turned its head and glared at them, then stood and once more began its slow shuffle toward the door. "Go," Abigail whispered, "now."

Timothy pushed away from the slab, barreling toward the mummy thing, his own arms outstretched in defense. As he came closer, he groaned. It had opened its jaw wide, prepared to chomp.

Timothy shoved his hand into the thing's mouth, gripping the bone like a door handle. But before he could yank it away, the creature bit down, hard. The pain was unlike anything Timothy had ever imagined. He tried to pull away, but the pain only increased. His fingers were now stuck inside the creature's mouth. It clasped his neck and began to squeeze.

Timothy stared into its empty eye sockets and saw his fate, lost forever in this hell of darkness. He kicked at the creature and managed to squeak, "Get . . . off . . . me!" The creature responded by dragging his face toward its own. It squeezed Timothy's neck harder and leaned closer.

"Abigail . . . help . . . ," he croaked.

His peripheral vision darkened. He was losing consciousness. He kicked at the creature's skinny legs again, but the corpse was surprisingly strong, and Timothy was getting weaker by the second.

Just then, light flashed next to his head, and something crashed into him. Timothy saw the creature fly against the far wall, before fresh darkness enveloped the room again. Abigail had sideswiped the corpse. She clutched Timothy's arm, dragging him away. When they reached the iron door, she whispered, "Are you okay?"

"What took you so long?" he said, rubbing his throat.

She punched him in the arm. Then she hugged him.

When she let go, he slumped to the floor. "Come on," she said, "stand up. It'll be back soon, and we need another plan."

Leaning against the door, they listened for any movement. To Timothy's surprise, he thought he heard a noise from the other side of the metal slab.

"Hello?" Zilpha called out. "Abigail? Timothy?"

44.

"In here!" they cried.

From the darkness where the creature had fallen, bones rattled. Timothy imagined it struggling to rise, shuffling through the pile of its former victim. "Hurry, Zilpha," he called.

"There's this wood plank," said the old woman. "It's heavy . . . but I think if I slide it . . ."

Timothy spun around, listening at the darkness, trying to get a sense of where the creature might now be. Both of his hands shrieked in pain, but he swung his arms out in front of him, in case the corpse came too close. Then something clattered to the ground outside. The slab moved toward them. A crack of light appeared, and Zilpha's worried face peered around the edge of the door.

"What is going on in there?" she said. Then, as she looked

over Abigail's shoulder, her eyes widened. "Good Lord! Pull!" Timothy and Abigail grabbed the edge of the door. They managed to open it about a foot, wide enough for them to slip into the larger cavern. Once outside, the kids pulled on the L-brackets, trying to shut the door again. It moved, but barely.

Suddenly, the ground shook. Dirt rained down from the ceiling. "What is that?" Timothy asked. Seconds later, it stopped.

"Let's just go," said Abigail, grabbing her grandmother's arm, turning back up the tunnel. Zilpha still carried the flashlight Timothy had given her. The other flashlight was gone. Harwood must have taken it. Zilpha's light bobbled and bounced off the rocks. Timothy followed close behind the other two, watching where Zilpha stepped in case she slipped. To his surprise, with Abigail's help, the old woman was able to slowly navigate the makeshift stairs.

The three of them diligently climbed the slope. Every few seconds, Timothy turned around to see if the creature was following, but all he could see behind them was dripping darkness. He didn't stare too long, though. Even after everything he'd seen that day, he couldn't bear one more glimpse at the monster's horrible face.

As they ascended, Zilpha spoke. "After you left me, Timothy, I slowly made my way down the stairs. Once inside the lighthouse, I found this passage."

"Are you okay?" said Timothy. "That staircase was enormous. And this tunnel . . ."

"Any discomfort I'm feeling now is nothing compared to what I would have felt if I'd done nothing," said Zilpha.

"Did you see Jack?" Timothy asked. "He was down here. He locked me in that room with Abigail."

Zilpha shook her head. "Either he's still down there, or he was hiding up in the lighthouse crow's nest when I came in. I never saw him come out."

"Dammit," said Abigail.

"What's wrong?" asked Timothy.

Zilpha shined the flashlight on a concrete wall directly ahead. They'd made it to the top of the tunnel, but the spiral staircase was gone. "That shaking we felt," she said. "Harwood closed the door. He *was* hiding from you upstairs, Gramma."

"What do we do now?" said Timothy.

"Think," said Zilpha. "Look around. When he built this place, Hesselius would have planned for some sort of escape."

"There," said Timothy, nodding at the far left side of the wall. "Shine the light."

Zilpha found the spot Timothy had mentioned. Where the blond concrete met the black bedrock, a small knob poked out from the wall.

"What is it?" said Abigail, leaning close.

"A dial combination," said Timothy. "Like on my school locker."

"Is it the same code from—?"

"No," Timothy interrupted Abigail. "Look. There are letters this time."

"But what's the code?" said Abigail. "Ugh, I'm so *sick* of this!"

A noise echoed up from the tunnel: the sound of something scraping against the rock.

Timothy didn't even have to think. "Righteousness, integrity, and sacrifice," he answered.

"If the dial works like our lockers," said Abigail, "maybe we need three letters. R. I. S.?"

"Try it," said Zilpha.

Abigail leaned forward and spun the dial. A few seconds later, the tunnel began to rumble, and a space appeared at the top of the wall. Soon the spiral staircase had lowered into the ground, revealing the opening to the lighthouse.

"Open, sesame," said Zilpha.

Abigail went first, helping her grandmother take each large step, followed by Timothy. The halogen lamp by the desk lit the lighthouse office with a dim glow. The engine whirred above their heads, and a few seconds later, the rotating light flashed from the hatch in the ceiling.

"Let's go," said Abigail.

"But we don't know where Harwood went," said Timothy.

"I don't care," said Abigail. "I'm not waiting around this place one more second to find out."

"We should at least call the police," said Zilpha, picking up the receiver on the desk. She held the cradle to her ear, then shook her head. "Dead."

"Come on," Abigail begged. Timothy opened the door. They were greeted by a strong, salty breeze. One by one, they crept out into the night. Timothy shut the door behind them. Standing on the gravel path, they glanced all around. The river lapped the rocks at the base of the outcropping behind them.

The flashing light was a beacon, showing them where they needed to go. "Do you think you can make it back up?" said Timothy, over his shoulder. Zilpha and Abigail followed him along the line of shrubbery in the direction of the cliffside.

"I'll try," said Zilpha.

"You'll fail," said a voice. Timothy turned around and found Jack standing several feet in front of him, blocking the long path that led to the stairs. He'd been waiting for them.

45.

To their right, the rock ledge dropped off to the river. To their left was the lighthouse. They had no way around Harwood. One slip, and over the cliff they'd fall.

"I don't know how you did it," said Harwood to Zilpha. "But I should have known. This is how you always beat your nemeses in those silly books."

Zilpha shook her head. "Mr. Harwood," she said evenly, as if to a small child, "those books are fiction. It seems to me that you've read them too many times. You're correct that in popular fiction, the bad guy rarely wins. But this is real life, and I don't believe that you're truly *bad*."

"Does that mean you're not truly good?"

"I can't answer that question," said Zilpha. "But if it helps, in real life, I never hurt anybody."

"Except for my father," said Harwood, adjusting his hat.

"What are you gonna do?" said Abigail, stepping between the man and her grandmother. "Throw us off the cliff?"

"Good guess," said Harwood. "Seems a bit disappointing after all the planning, to have to resort to something so simple. But I suppose I might receive some sort of satisfaction knowing that I handled it myself." He took another step, forcing them all backward toward the edge of the rock.

"There is one thing I do not understand, Mr. Harwood," said Zilpha. Timothy could tell she was trying to stall. "Why not just keep the jawbone to yourself? After you located it down in the crypt that your father built, you could've hurt us without putting it in the museum."

Jack glared at her. "Four words: Zelda Kite, Youth Sleuth."

"But Zelda was just a character in a book," said Timothy. "Mrs. Kindred isn't—"

"Mrs. Kindred did the research. Mrs. Kindred found me. Zelda Kite may have only been a character in a book, but her characteristics were based on Zilpha Kindred's *inhuman* interest in finding answers to questions that don't have answers. I see it runs in the family." Harwood nodded at Abigail, who grunted angrily at him. "I brought the jawbone to the museum collection because if I didn't, then how else would Zelda have learned what I was going to do? My plan changed once I learned of Abigail's existence. Ah, but what would be the point in getting revenge on someone if they had no idea they'd been part of it? A missing granddaughter is a sad story, but to find out that the story has a connection with her own history, well, that changes things, doesn't it? I knew Zelda would play detective. I *let* you find out it was me."

"What if she'd stopped you?" said Timothy.

"But she didn't." Harwood blinked, his face a total blank. "And she won't."

"You're ill," said Zilpha.

"At least I'm no fool," he countered. Harwood took another step, forcing them backward, past the lighthouse door to the river, until they were all crowded at the outcropping's far edge. Timothy glanced around, looking for some other way out. The river rushed past sharp rocks twenty feet below.

"If we fall, I'll take you with us," said Abigail. "I swear."

The old man laughed. "The girl's got sass," Harwood told Zilpha. "But that hasn't stopped me yet." He paused, thinking, then said, "No, that's not quite how it goes. . . ."

Timothy heard sirens coming over the Taft Bridge. Seconds later, on the cliff near his mother's car, flashing lights appeared. The police. His father must have come home to discover his house a disaster, his son missing, and his wife's car stolen. Surely, he'd alerted the authorities. Or maybe it had been Mrs. Mendelson. . . .

"You're too late," said Timothy. "The police will help us."

Harwood shrugged. "They're awfully far away." He took another step forward.

Behind him, the lighthouse door opened. Outlined in the

halogen glow, a tall, thin shadow fell across the gravel path. Harwood did not notice, but the rest of them saw it clearly.

"Would it make any difference if I said I'm sorry?" the old woman asked, rushing. "Because I am. I'm very, very sorry you had to lose your father. That was not my intention."

"Sorry?" said Harwood, surprised.

"Yes," said Zilpha, frantic. "I feel sorry about what happened every day of my life. To your family. To Delia. To everyone else involved in this whole disaster."

"I . . ." Harwood seemed stunned, as if this was one development he truly had not considered possible. Timothy almost felt sorry for him—in a totally pathetic, "he still deserves everything that's coming to him" sort of way.

Behind Harwood, the corpse was headed toward the small group huddled at the cliff edge. Its hair whipped against its face in the wind. Its rags rustled like a tattered flag, raised after a fiery battle. Lifting its arms, the creature shuffled forward along the path. Harwood was oblivious to its approach.

The creature came closer. If it reached past Harwood for them, Timothy was prepared to leap into the river. We *might* survive, he thought.

Harwood came at them. Flashlights arched like shooting stars at the top the stairs. The police. "Down here!" cried Timothy.

Harwood turned around in surprise.

Zilpha whispered, "Timothy, no!"

Before Timothy could respond, Harwood had spun on them, a wicked gleam in his eye. He'd seen the creature, which was less than ten feet away. "Well, well," he said. "Look who's awake." He stepped aside, off the path. Now nothing separated the trio from the shuffling corpse. It opened its mouth.

The flashlights had begun the long descent down the stairs.

Zilpha hugged Abigail tightly. "Abigail . . . Timothy . . . close your eyes."

But Timothy did not close his eyes. The corpse stopped along the path, turned, and faced Mr. Harwood. The old man's smile dropped away. "What are you doing?" he said. "Get the girl!" The corpse reached for Harwood's throat. He tried to duck away, but the creature was too quick. It grabbed the old man with its bony fingers, then jerked Harwood's face close to its own. The corpse attached its mouth to the old man's in a revolting kiss. Harwood opened his eyes wide as he realized what was happening to him. He struggled to push the thing away, but the corpse lifted the old man off the ground. Harwood emitted a pained howl. Timothy wanted to believe that, if it was Delia's soul that still faintly charged the corpse, this was her version of revenge.

A harsh sucking noise came from the direction of the struggle. Timothy watched in revulsion as Harwood's skin became black and shriveled, as if burning under an invisible flame. The man's wide eyes sank into their sockets and disappeared. Where his mouth met the corpse, a cold light began to glow. Harwood's gray overcoat seemed to deflate as, bit by bit, the body inside crumbled to the ground. Terrified, Timothy finally covered his eyes. Something crunched into the bushes near the lighthouse. A few seconds later, the only sound he heard was the rushing of the water against the rocks below. When he looked again, the path appeared to be empty.

"Follow me," said Zilpha, stepping toward the lighthouse. Several feet ahead, two piles of bones littered the ground. One pile lay inside the large gray overcoat. The other was barely covered by tattered black rags.

"Is it over?" Timothy asked.

"The corpse . . . fed," said Abigail quietly.

46.

The flashlights finally bobbed at the base of the stairs, a hundred yards away. The police were running toward them.

"Are you folks all right?" An officer blocked their path, shining her flashlight at them.

Zilpha swiftly stepped in front of the piles of bones. "We are now," she answered.

Zilpha held Abigail's hand and spoke with the officers. Standing several feet back, Timothy glanced down at what was left of the two bodies.

In the creature's skull, something small glimmered much brighter than before. He bent down to get a closer look. Deep inside the jawbone's single sharp black tooth, a golden light flickered. Remembering the myths of the chaos cult, he imagined that this new glow was the soul of Mr. Harwood. The bone had been charged, its power rejuvenated. If the scary things Timothy had experienced this past week had been the time-weakened results of the corpse's long-ago last meal, a fresh soul might make the jawbone infinitely more dangerous. Reaching out with his one barely able hand, Timothy poked the jawbone, almost expecting the skull to clamp its mouth shut. But the life had gone out of the monster. He figured it would spark only if the corpse was returned to the crypt, and he was pretty sure that wasn't going to happen.

Quickly, Timothy plucked the jawbone from the creature. It came away easily. Zilpha would probably still want to destroy it. He shoved it into his jacket pocket for her. Then, staring at the gray remains buried under the nearby overcoat, Timothy had an idea.

After nearly fifteen minutes of questions, the police finally led Zilpha, Abigail, and Timothy back up the long flight of stairs.

When it came to their story, Timothy and Abigail had followed Zilpha's lead. She had explained to the police that Mr. Harwood had kidnapped her granddaughter and held her in the vault underneath the lighthouse. She mentioned that they might find another body down there.

"Did you see which direction this Mr. Harwood ran?" asked one officer.

"No," Zilpha answered, "he simply disappeared."

The police examined the bones scattered across the gravel

path. Timothy knew it would only be a matter of time before they discovered Harwood's wallet or car keys or something to identify him. Then the mystery would begin for *them*.

As for Timothy, Abigail, and Zilpha, they finally had their answers.

At the top of the stairs, Timothy found his father pacing. When he noticed Timothy, he raced forward and lifted his son into his arms. He squeezed Timothy so hard that for a second, Timothy couldn't breathe.

His father told him that when he'd gotten home from Saturday-evening services at the church, he'd found the front window smashed by the planter, the garage door completely destroyed, and his wife's car stolen. He'd immediately called the police, worried that Timothy might be in trouble. The police had already received reports of a boy driving a car west across the bridge.

"What about the rest of the house?" Timothy asked, trying to change the subject.

"What do you mean?" said his dad. "The rest of the house is fine . . . isn't it?"

"Oh . . . yeah," said Timothy. "I was just wondering." He'd known the jawbone's curse had created the dragon, but until now, he hadn't known where the line between fantasy and reality had been drawn. When it came to the curse, the trick lay in telling the difference between the two. The dragon had been imaginary; Timothy driving the car through the garage door, however, had been very real. The Nightmarys at Harwood's house had been imaginary; the incomplete corpse below the lighthouse had been genuine. But in the moment, Timothy had been helpless to stop his imagination from taking control. He racked his brain, trying to think of what he could tell his father about why he'd taken the car. But before he had a chance to think, his father gasped.

"Your hand is swollen!"

"Yeah. It kinda hurts."

"Can you move it?"

Timothy shook his head.

"We've got to get you to the emergency room," said Mr. July, glancing around for an officer. "What happened down there?"

"Um . . . That's hard to explain."

47.

A few hours later, Timothy sat on his bed, staring out the window. The stars in the sky were beginning to fade as dawn became a faint idea above the city along the eastern horizon. He was exhausted and had tried several times since arriving home from the hospital to lie down and sleep, but his brain raced and kept him awake. Every creak in the house, every popping pipe and boiler hum, made Timothy brace himself for a new strange attack.

Abigail and Zilpha had accompanied Timothy and his father to the emergency room. While they all waited, Mr. July and Zilpha continued their discussion with the police. Making sure no one was watching, Timothy reached into his pocket and pulled out what he'd taken from the gravel path. He discreetly handed it to Abigail and whispered, "Your grandmother's been looking for this for such a long time. I didn't think we should leave it there."

"Oh my God," said Abigail. "I was so happy to be out of that place, I forgot." Tentatively, she took the bone, then gave Timothy a curious look. "She'll destroy it immediately."

"I hope so," said Timothy.

They were silent for a few seconds; then Abigail quickly hugged him. "Thank you," she said, blushing. "You know . . . for rescuing me."

"But we rescued each other," Timothy answered.

She rolled her eyes. "*You* are a cheeseball."

In his bedroom, his hands didn't hurt so much anymore; the pain medication was strong. The doctors had taken X-rays. A nurse had put a cast on his left hand—the one with the bite. She'd wrapped his right hand tightly in a beige bandage. Using the more flexible of the two, Timothy lifted his pillow.

On the striped blue sheets, beside the bed's headboard, lay the real jawbone. The single sharp black tooth jutted from the brown horseshoe-shaped object. As he stared at it, the golden glimmer inside the tooth grew brighter, and he was filled with a new sensation, something he couldn't name. It almost felt like a voice was talking to him through a long-distance phone line. Timothy couldn't understand the words, but he understood the meaning deep underneath them. This was the reason he'd done what he'd done back at the lighthouse.

Standing on the gravel path, Zilpha and Abigail had been busy speaking with the police. Without thinking, Timothy had bent down and snatched the corpse's jawbone, making it "incomplete" again, slipping it into his jacket pocket. He was about to stand, when instead, he reached out and took Mr. Harwood's gray jawbone as well; it had come away from the empty skull with a soft, brittle snap. Clutching a handful of gravel from under his feet, Timothy swiftly sorted through the black stones, found one of appropriate size, and replaced one of Harwood's teeth with it.

The new jawbone was a fairly convincing fake. Timothy quickly stood and slipped the small piece of Harwood into his opposite pocket.

Harwood's jaw had been the "relic" he'd handed to Abigail in the emergency room. He was certain, at this point, that Zilpha had done something to make it disappear for good.

Timothy stroked the real jawbone with his exposed left thumb. The bone felt rough, papery, impossibly light. The energy contained inside it gave him a jolt, and he drew away, frightened by what he'd done. He wasn't even sure what he planned to do with the object; he only knew that he had to have it.

The sky grew brighter. Looking east, Timothy wondered what his mother was doing at the moment. Was she sitting beside Ben, holding his hand, praying? What would Timothy tell her when she arrived home? What would she tell him?

Without warning, Timothy was flooded with anger. He was angry with Stuart for being so cruel. He was angry with his parents for making him keep secrets from his best friend. He was angry with his brother for volunteering for such a dangerous job in the first place. He was especially angry with the people across the ocean who'd planted the explosives along the side of the road—so angry, in fact, that his tears blinded him.

In the past month, Timothy felt like he had given so much of himself away. He'd stood by, done what he'd been told, tried to be a good person, and yet the horrors had continued to unfold, endlessly. Timothy was sick of doing what was right. Wasn't it about time for someone to pay him back?

The articles in the New Starkham newspaper had revealed that Christian Hesselius had wanted to use the jawbone as a weapon of revenge.

Now Timothy had the power to do the same.

The jawbone seemed so small, unassuming. But the dark tooth was a different story. Looking closer, Timothy understood it was not of this world. Sculpted black metal. Hollow, porous, almost like filigree. Something that might have fallen from space. Like a meteorite. That sparkle of light inside it teased him again.

Do it, said the Chaos voice.

Make them pay.

Put an end to it all.

Ben would thank you.

You'll be a hero.

Using the exposed fingertips of his left hand, Timothy unraveled the bandage from his right. The skin underneath was black and blue, but when he wiggled his fingers, he felt no pain. He picked up the jawbone. Again, a jolt of energy rushed through his body. But this time, instead of shrinking away, Timothy clutched the bone as if it were a sword.

Names and faces of people he knew raced through his mind. His classmates, his grandparents, the teachers at his school, his swim team. He could hear their thoughts, see their memories. Several of them lingered longer than others, and he felt a question tug at him, somewhere deep inside, during these brief moments. All he would have to do was say yes, and it would be done. But Timothy did not say yes. He waited as more and more identities came at him, until he saw faces of people he had never met. In his head, he heard the strange voice whisper their names. People who lived across an ocean. People who had hurt his brother.

All he had to do was say yes.

It would be done.

Do it, demanded the voice. *Do it.*

Timothy opened his mouth and began to speak.

The doorbell rang.

Timothy dropped the jawbone.

Immediately, he felt as if a thousand-pound blanket had

been removed from his shoulders. He wasn't quite sure what had been happening. Before he had a chance to think, the doorbell rang again.

Placing the pillow over the jawbone, Timothy slipped out of bed. The hardwood floor was chilly. He opened his bedroom door, glancing down the hall toward the back of the house. His parents' bedroom door remained closed.

The bell rang again. Who the heck could be here at such an hour? Cautiously, Timothy crept down the hallway, leaning over the banister, trying to catch a glimpse through the front door's window. Standing at the top of the stairs, he saw a tall, thin silhouette on the other side of the gauzy curtain.

Curious, Timothy tentatively crept halfway down the steps. The doorknob rattled, then the visitor knocked. His heart felt like it might pop, but Timothy continued down the stairs. When he finally reached the bottom step, the visitor smashed the glass.

Timothy screamed and fell backward, landing halfway down the stairs. He watched, paralyzed, as a thin brown arm reached through the broken window for the lock. Its skeletal fingers turned the knob, and slowly, the front door creaked open.

The corpse stood in the entrance, the dawn lighting the sky in the distance. The creature's white hair lay limp across its skull. The bottom half of its face was missing. Its empty eye sockets were barely visible, but Timothy felt their blackness dig into his chest. The corpse clutched at the wood frame and dragged its feet across the threshold.

"This is *your* fault," said the creature, its voice like rags. "*You* did this to me."

"I—I didn't do anything!" Timothy cried, scrambling backward up the steps. "I'll give it back. I swear."

The creature shuffled toward him, wrinkling the throw rug on the floor. When it had made it halfway through the foyer, it cried, "Make them stop!"

Timothy shouted, *"DAD!"*

"Tell them to leave me alone!" said the creature, raising its hands to its face.

"I—I don't know what you're—"

Upstairs, a door opened. "Timothy, what's going on?" Seconds later, Timothy's father dashed down the stairs to where Timothy was sprawled. Glancing up, his father noticed they weren't alone. "Who . . . who are you?" he asked.

Who are you? thought Timothy. Does it matter?

"It's his fault." The creature pointed at Timothy. "I told him to throw those jars away. But he keeps bringing them back. He sneaks into my house and puts them in my bed. The things inside pretend to be dead, but they're not. They watch me. *He* tells them to!"

"Sir, please . . ."

Jars? thought Timothy. His father was seeing something

he was not. This was another illusion. Timothy fought to see through it. The creature rippled, then became solid again.

"Why don't you sit down?" said Timothy's father evenly. He stepped over Timothy, cautiously making his way down the rest of the stairs. "Tell me what you want."

"Dad, don't get any closer!"

"I know you," whispered Timothy's father. "We met at the school."

"The school . . . ," said Timothy. It suddenly made sense.

"Isn't this your teacher?" asked Timothy's father. "Crane, right?" A moment later, the corpse changed shape and became a sad-looking man wearing purple plaid pajamas.

"Please," said Mr. Crane, collapsing to the floor, "just tell your son to stop."

Standing above the man on the rug, Timothy's father looked up and said, "Call the police."

48.

Five minutes later, Timothy stood in the house's front doorway, watching his father comfort his teacher. The two men sat on the porch's top step. Mr. Crane hung his head and wouldn't stop crying, even as Timothy's father awkwardly patted his back.

As soon as Timothy handed the phone over to his father, he realized the mistake he'd made earlier that night. When he'd taken the jawbone from the corpse instead of handing it over to Zilpha to be destroyed, the curse had continued. Everything he'd just seen had been part of it. The incomplete corpse had not come looking for him, but his teacher had. Like Stuart, Mr. Crane had no idea how to control his own fears. For some reason, the teacher blamed Timothy for what was happening to him, just as Stuart had blamed Abigail for the horrors he'd been seeing. Timothy understood now the close relationship that existed between Chaos and Blame. Christian Hesselius's ancient tribe understood it too. They had exploited the power of their mysterious black metal, and most likely had destroyed themselves because of it. This weapon did more than merely materialize people's fear; it turned them against each other. It made them blind.

Now Timothy saw what he must do.

Carefully avoiding the broken glass at his feet, Timothy stepped out onto the front porch. The sky had turned purple. The light caught wispy clouds on the horizon and painted them pale pink. It would be another beautiful day. "Mr. Crane?" said Timothy. The man would not look at him. "I just want you to know, those things in the jars won't be watching you anymore."

His father turned around and glared at Timothy. "Don't provoke him," he whispered. Glancing down the street, he said, almost to himself, "Where is the damn ambulance?" The street was quiet. Everyone in the neighborhood was asleep; Timothy finally felt tired enough to do the same. But there was one thing he needed to complete first.

Climbing down the front steps, Timothy said, "I'll be right back." He ran toward the garage. He stepped over pieces of the demolished door. Half a day ago, this building had been on fire. Timothy blinked away the memory and focused on his father's toolbox, which lay on the floor against the rear wall. Buried at the bottom was a heavy hammer.

As he lifted the tool from the box, Timothy thought of Christian Hesselius and his son Jack. They had been his age once. They'd probably thought of themselves as good people. Maybe they had treasured the same things Timothy did. Family. Friends. Home. But then Christian's and Jack's lives had changed dramatically, just as Timothy's had this month. He realized the power of the jawbone upstairs. He thought of how easily he had almost given into the bliss of its persuasiveness.

It was the bone that had taken control of those men and planted a dark seed in their minds. It was the bone that had turned them into monsters. And it was the bone that needed to be destroyed.

This should do it, Timothy thought, clutching the handle of the hammer. He made his way back to the driveway and was about to cross the small path that led to the back door, when he noticed small, dew-wet footprints going up the back steps. The door was already open a crack. Had someone snuck inside?

Timothy clutched the hammer in his right hand, which had begun to ache. The medication was wearing off. He ignored the pain. Using his elbow, he nudged the door the rest of the way open.

"H-hello?" he called into the house.

Timothy crept into the empty kitchen, listening for an answer.

The curse was still alive. Anything he encountered now

might only be an illusion. Even though he'd gotten good at handling it, breaking the illusion still took work.

The ceiling creaked. There was someone upstairs.

Or was there?

Timothy wasn't sure of anything anymore. He quickly crossed through the kitchen and peered into the hallway. Through the front door, he saw his father still sitting with

Mr. Crane on the front steps. Neither of them seemed to notice anything wrong. Timothy climbed the stairs, taking two at a time.

His bedroom door at the front of the house was closed. "Hello?" he called again. After a few seconds, he tightened his grip on the hammer and trudged down the hall. When he was halfway there, his door swung open. Timothy froze. "Abigail?" She stood in his doorway, wearing a sheepish expression. "What are you doing?"

She licked her lips. After a few seconds, she answered. "I think the question is, what are *you* doing, Timothy?" She shifted the cuff of her sweatshirt sleeve slightly. He noticed what she held in her fist, what she was trying to hide. The jawbone.

His mouth went dry. "I . . . made a mistake," he said. "I'm sorry I lied. Yes, so I took the jawbone, but I need to finish this now." He raised the hammer. "We can do it together."

Abigail shook her head. "How am I supposed to trust you?"

Timothy blushed. He felt awful.

"This thing is powerful," said Abigail, glancing at what she held in her fist. "I can feel it now. I don't know if you're strong enough to resist what it wants you to do."

"And what would that be?"

"To use it," said Abigail. She squinted at him, her eyes like lasers. "You were going to use it, Timothy. I know you were." Timothy didn't know what to say. She was right. "After everything we've gone through? After everything we've seen?"

She stepped toward him, as if she had the power to hurt him, as if she might truly want to. She didn't look quite right. She'd always been intense, but even when they'd fought, horribly, she'd never appeared to be so . . . self-righteous.

"I know," said Timothy. "I came back up here to smash that thing. If you don't believe me, then do it yourself." Timothy held out the hammer to Abigail. She took another step toward him but ignored his offering.

"Gramma's the only one I can trust with this. She's the one who should destroy it."

"But . . . how do I know that *you're* strong enough to resist what it wants?" Timothy asked.

Abigail stepped toward him, her mouth pulled up in a strange smile.

He suddenly understood what was happening here. His skin went ice cold. "Abigail, I think you should go," he whispered. He tried to step past her toward his bedroom. "Go do whatever you need to do."

She blocked his way. "No," she spat. She would not let him pass. In fact, she reached behind her and shut his bedroom door. "You're coming with me."

"Abigail . . ." He didn't know what to think anymore. All he knew was that he needed to get into his bedroom. He had to check under his pillow. The jawbone was still lying there, hiding from him, and was not in fact in Abigail's fist.

Abigail shouted, then raised her hand as if to strike him. Timothy cringed against the banister, then stumbled backward toward his parents' bedroom. Abigail didn't look like herself anymore. Her black hair had grown past her shoulders and had begun to show white. Long strands of it had caught on her face, a soiled veil. Her sweatshirt began to separate, falling into tatters of string toward the floor, looking like dirty pieces of lacy cobweb.

Behind her, Timothy's bedroom door burst open. Timothy gasped. Girls now crowded at the entry as if trying to catch a glimpse of what was about to happen. The Nightmarys had returned. The upstairs was suddenly filled with their singsong chatter. They watched as Abigail continued her slow approach. Some of the girls scratched at the wooden doorframe with their long fingernails, as if trying to sharpen them.

Abigail's scream had turned into a siren wail, so loud, Timothy felt as if his eardrums might burst. She came closer and closer. The hammer slipped out of Timothy's hand as he turned around and dashed toward his parents' bedroom.

Once inside, he slammed the door shut and locked it. He stared at the dark wood, listening to the scrambling, scratching noises that were coming from the other side, out in the hallway.

Abigail was not here. She was probably at home, in bed. What was happening now was caused by the curse. The jawbone was trying to protect itself. Timothy knew it would do anything to survive—make him see whatever scared him most. And right now, that was losing his friend, having her turn against him.

Again, Abigail's statement popped into his head: *I know they'll kill you . . . because* I'm terrified *that they will.* Before, Timothy had believed that wasn't possible, that the curse had merely created illusions, that the only real danger he'd been in was from himself. But now, if this was to be a battle for survival, Timothy wondered if the jawbone might try to raise the stakes a bit.

Little tricks, he remembered. Zilpha's advice. If the Nightmarys were what the jawbone had sent to stop him, then he needed to find a way to beat the Nightmarys once and for all.

The door rattled. Screeching, the creatures on the other side sounded like they might just be able to tear it down.

Timothy glanced around for something, anything, that might stop them. But when he turned toward the darkest corner of the room near his parents' closet, he noticed a tall patch of cobweb. A dark shape shifted behind it. The Nightmarys were finding another way in.

Before he could think to stop himself, Timothy leapt at the web. He tore the patch away from the ceiling and the walls. It came away as easily as the spiderwebs that he and Stuart sometimes found stretched across their front porches. Timothy's arms were now covered with a strange sticky sub-

stance, but he quickly brushed most of it off. The long strands fell to the floor in a dingy lump. The dark shifting shape that had been forming behind the web faded away into shadow, then disappeared altogether. Timothy spun but stumbled against the closet door when he saw another patch of web appear across the bedroom next to his parents' bed.

Turning toward the closet, Timothy grappled with the knob, then swung the door open. Little tricks. There had to be something in here he could use to stop this. Rows of hanging clothes stared back at him. All useless. Then, way up on the top shelf, something caught his eye. His mother kept cleaning supplies in here. Jumping as high as he could reach, Timothy managed to catch the tip of a feather duster between his bandaged fingers. He turned around.

One of the creepy girls stood behind him, her screech piercing his eardrums, her claws reaching forward as if to tear him apart.

Before she came too close, he swiped at her face. Using the duster as if it were a sword, Timothy waved his weapon until her cobweb veil became entangled in the feathers. After a few swipes, all that was left of her head was a cloud of dust motes. Between her collarbone, a black hole coughed and wheezed, and a musty stench burped forth. Disgusted, Timothy covered his mouth. The girl shuddered; then, to Timothy's surprise, she simply unraveled into longs pieces of string and lace and dirt, which piled at his feet and disappeared.

Outside, the scratching grew louder. Timothy moved cautiously toward the bedroom door. He counted to three, then managed to swing it open. The girls rushed him the same way they had at the house on Ash Tree Lane, but now Timothy was prepared. He ducked and swung down the landing, smashing and slashing his way past them. The feather duster was his own Excalibur. With each step he took, pieces of the phantom girls piled up on the floor behind him. Every time he took off one of their heads, another girl shrieked in surprise and ducked away. It was as if the curse couldn't believe he'd figured out a way to beat it.

He quickly made his way down the landing toward his own bedroom. Slipping inside, he slammed the door shut and moved his desk chair in front of it, locking the rest of the Nightmarys outside. Panting, he turned toward his bed. Clutching the feather duster painfully, he approached his pillow with caution, as if another nightmare might leap out from underneath his sheets to attack him. He managed to lift the pillow away from his mattress. The jawbone still lay inconspicuously underneath. Something inside the black tooth glowed violently, angrily. Timothy was afraid to touch the thing, as if whatever control it had exerted over him earlier might take hold once more. Using his weapon, Timothy simply knocked the small object to the cold wooden floor, where it eventually rattled into stillness beside his nightstand. He dropped the duster. Then, grabbing his thick history textbook from his nearby desk, Timothy knelt down next to the bone. As he raised the book over his head, Timothy thought, This is for you, Ben. Then he brought his arms down as hard as he could.

GRADUATION

DAY

ENDINGS

[From the *New Starkham Record*—Obituaries]

BYRON FLANDERS—FORMER NEW STARKHAM DISTRICT ATTORNEY

. . . Mr. Flanders had recently suffered a heart attack and passed away at New Starkham Hospital before his surgery . . . Known best for his unflappable work ethic and strong personality, Flanders strove tirelessly to protect the citizens of New Starkham from those whom he had once referred to as "The Real Monsters." He is survived by his wife and three children.

☆ ☆ ☆

Percival Ankh closed the newspaper with a shudder. He hadn't thought of his old friend Flanders in quite some time. "Do you want to attend the service?" his wife asked.

"I don't think so," he answered quietly. It had been during a dinner with Flanders many years ago that the topic of Christian Hesselius's abandoned office had been raised. Flanders had been the prosecutor in the case and had asked if his friend believed in ghosts. That had been the seed that had sparked Percival's fear of the old professor—and the subsequent raising of the wall that had sealed off the room in the library.

After the horrible experience at the birthday party several weeks ago, Percival wanted once more to forget the old stories that had haunted him for so long. He had good reason to forget too. At the restaurant, his son had found Ankh lying on the bathroom floor, weeping. The old man never told anyone what he'd seen in there.

"Are you sure?" asked his wife. "He was your friend."

Getting up from the dining room table, he tossed the newspaper onto the floor and said, "I'd rather just stay here with you, my dear." Carefully bending down, he kissed his wife's cheek.

She smiled and patted his head. "Whatever you like," she answered.

* * *

When Emma Huppert came home from the beach, she threw her towel onto the back of a chair in the kitchen. Bill had left the mail on the table. Lying on top of the pile was a letter. Emma gasped when she noticed the return address. She hadn't spoken to Zilpha Kindred in years. She quickly tore open the envelope. Inside was a newspaper clipping—the obituary of the prosecutor in her sister's case, along with a brief note scrawled on a scrap of paper.

Emma, I thought you might find this to be of interest. Do with it what you will. Much love, Zilpha.

Tears welled in Emma's eyes. Over the past couple of months, ever since Delia began appearing to her, she'd been meaning to call the one old friend back in New Starkham who might understand what the experience meant; however, she'd been too frightened to even speak of it to anyone at all.

But recently, Delia had suddenly stopped "visiting."

Emma prayed every day that Delia was at peace now. She knew in her heart that her sister didn't blame her for what had happened long ago. It had been none of their faults. And despite the horrific vision in the Wal-Mart dressing room, Emma still thought about her sister every time she put on her new bathing suit and stepped into the cold Atlantic to go for her now-daily swims. She wished, with her entire soul, that Delia could have joined her.

* * *

On a Tuesday morning at the beginning of May, Zilpha Kindred's washing machine finally died. By that afternoon, two men had delivered a brand-new one. Three people were going to be living in the apartment from now on, and it would not do to simply keep repairing the old clunker. Zilpha was no longer willing to use the one in the basement.

Later that evening, with little Hepzibah at her feet, Zilpha decided to test out the contraption. The nightmare laundry experience of two months ago seemed like a dream, the memory of it fading even more quickly than Zilpha had hoped it would. Thank goodness.

As the old woman loaded the basket and poured in the detergent, she thought about Abigail and Timothy and how the surreal events of the past few weeks might linger in their memories, or grow, or change. Zilpha was surprised that the children had been able to get out of bed that week. She figured that children must have a natural resilience after these sorts of things. It's later, she thought, after time and trouble and life itself have worn down our resistance and the ghosts come back to haunt, that we must find ways of tricking ourselves into finally subduing them. It was possible, she now knew.

Zilpha closed the lid with a bang and cranked the silver knob. The water ran and the machine began to hum. "Come on, Hep," she said, heading down the hallway toward the kitchen. "This thing can take care of itself."

49.

Timothy waited at the edge of the bridge, watching the traffic cross the river. Cars, packed with boxes, books, and small pieces of furniture, sped through the green light. Down the hill, on the campus, the ceremony wasn't over yet, but the college students, underclassmen mostly, were already leaving New Starkham. It wasn't fair. He wished his own classes ended at the beginning of May. If the past week had felt like a millennium, the month and a half left before summer break would be an eternity.

Mr. Crane hadn't come back to school. Word had spread that he was "taking a sabbatical" for the remainder of the year. Timothy didn't exactly understand what that meant. People said the man had had a nervous breakdown.

Timothy knew what had really happened, and though he knew it wasn't his fault Mr. Crane had tried to break into his house a week ago, he felt strangely guilty about it. None of what happened had been Mr. Crane's fault either. When he'd heard Randy and Brian making fun of their absent teacher during history class on Friday, Timothy had to keep his hands under his desk to refrain from whacking their skulls with his cast. If the boys knew what any of them had been through, they wouldn't have snickered. However, they quickly changed

the subject when the substitute entered the classroom and reminded the class that their museum projects were still due the next week.

Timothy had glanced at Abigail. They'd already decided on a different artifact than the painting. Instead, they picked one of the ancient cow-femur toothbrushes—less creepy. From her seat two rows away, Abigail had returned a slight smile.

Carla had raised her hand. "My partner's been absent. Maybe I should work with someone else."

The sub smiled. "Stuart Chen will return next Monday. You'll still have time to finish." Carla sighed—not the answer she'd been hoping for.

Stuart had come home from the hospital the previous Sunday, the same day Mr. Crane had been admitted. Timothy stopped by the Chens' a couple of times after school that week. Stuart didn't mention any more of what he'd said at the hospital, and Timothy didn't ask. Mrs. Chen doted on the two of them, glad to have her boys together again. She cooked and chatted and asked silly questions about Timothy's feelings and assured him that he could tell her anything if he needed to. Obviously, Mrs. Chen had learned about Ben's injuries. Only a few weeks earlier, he'd believed that his parents might be able to keep quiet such a big secret. Now he knew that some secrets speak themselves aloud after a while.

"Hey!"

Timothy was startled out of his daydream. Across the highway, Abigail waved. He waved back.

Seeing Abigail gave Timothy goose bumps. He hadn't been sure she would show up. On the phone, when she'd asked him what this was all about, he'd said he'd rather tell her in person. She'd gotten quiet but, after a moment, agreed to meet him where he'd asked.

The stoplight changed, and Abigail crossed. "Hey," she said again. "You walk all the way here?"

Timothy nodded. "My dad left to pick up my mom at the airport. He said they needed some alone time on the ride home. I don't blame them."

"That's generous of you," said Abigail, crossing her arms and smirking. She added softly, "Then Ben's really awake. He's coming home?"

"Eventually, he will." Timothy popped a huge smile. "At least that's what they tell me."

Abigail gave him a quick hug. "That's amazing," she said. "He's so lucky."

"Yeah," he said. "He is." The army was admitting Ben to a veterans' hospital in Rhode Island for rehabilitation, not far from New Starkham. "It'll be nice to see him. For real. Finally." Actually, Timothy was terrified at the prospect.

"So, are we just going to stand here?" Abigail asked. "Or are you going to tell me what this is all about?"

Now Timothy was even more terrified. He winced as he reached into the pocket of his jeans with his bandaged right hand, making sure the small warm piece of metal against his leg was still there. "Let's walk," he said.

Abigail seemed surprised when Timothy did not cross back toward Edgehill Road but turned toward the bridge instead. Still, she managed to follow close behind as he trundled along the broken sidewalk. Several minutes later, they were halfway across the bridge. "We're not getting ourselves into another sticky situation, are we?" Abigail added, "'Cause I'd like to be prepared. . . ."

Timothy stopped and leaned against the rusted green railing, staring north, up the river. The sun had passed the sky's midpoint. The wind whipped his hair away from his forehead.

The lighthouse sat below, upon its outcropping on the western shore, oblivious to the secrets buried within. The water crashed against its rough rocks in swirling pools and white-capped waves. Timothy wondered if a place was capable of knowing its own history. Like the people in it, New Starkham still had plenty of secrets.

"Timothy?" said Abigail, touching his shoulder. "It's over, you know."

Timothy glanced at her. "That's the thing I wanted to tell you. . . . It's not."

"What do you mean, it's not?" asked Abigail, clutching the rusted green railing. Now the wind plastered her black bangs to her forehead. Her light red roots were just barely beginning to show. "Have you seen something again?"

"No," said Timothy, glancing at the water. "Nothing like that." She waited for him to speak. "Abigail . . . I did something last weekend . . . something really horrible. And now I think I'm paying for it."

"What did you do?" she said quietly.

Reaching into his pocket, Timothy pulled out the black piece of metal. He pinched it between his thumb and forefinger, holding it up for Abigail to see. Struggling to speak, he said, "I lied to you."

Timothy told Abigail his story—how he'd taken both bones but switched out Mr. Harwood's for the real one. He told her what he'd meant to do with it. He told her about Mr. Crane knocking on his front door, and what happened later when he went back to his room to destroy the object, how he thought he'd seen her appear in his bedroom, followed by the Nightmarys, as the jawbone's curse fought to protect itself from being broken.

Abigail simply watched him as he spoke, her face unreadable. When he finished his story, he thought she might punch him in the eye. Instead, she plucked the metal shard from his fingers and examined it more closely.

"It's not glowing," she said. Timothy nodded. "So, it's *over,*" she added, with finality. "Whatever was inside this chip is gone."

"You really believe that?" Timothy asked.

"Can't you feel it?"

"I guess so."

Abigail handed the piece back to Timothy and sighed. "I have a confession too," she said, staring at him. "At the hospital, I knew you were lying."

"You knew I gave you the wrong bone?" Timothy shook his head in disbelief. Abigail smiled. "But why'd you let me do it?" he asked.

"I don't know," she said. "Maybe it was the curse. Maybe not. I guess, deep down, I thought you needed it for something."

"I thought I did too," said Timothy, palming the tooth. Quickly, he turned his hand over. The black chip fell, turning and glinting in the sunlight, until it disappeared into the dark water beneath them. "But I was wrong."

They strolled back toward New Starkham. The cars

continued to whiz past. Every now and again, someone honked, a student happy to be leaving. They were almost at the part of the bridge that stretched over the campus parking lot when Abigail froze. She glanced over her shoulder at the lighthouse. "I'll be back," she said. "Wait for me." She turned and ran in the direction from which they'd come. Once she was over the water again, she reached into her back pocket. Something silver glinted in her hand as she waved it over her head. Then, closing her eyes, she threw the lighter as hard as she could. Like the tooth, it faded away, then disappeared into the Little Husketomic.

When she returned to where Timothy stood, he said, "Hey, I thought you needed that."

"I thought I did too," Abigail echoed. "But I was wrong."

Once they reached the intersection at Edgehill Road, she said, "Come over, if you want. Mom said we could order a pizza, and Gramma wants to listen to my grandfather's records with us." She shrugged. "I know it sounds kind of boring, compared to everything else we've been through. . . ."

"That doesn't sound boring," Timothy said, smiling. "Actually, that sounds like fun."

ACKNOWLEDGMENTS

Many thanks to my friends and family who supported this story from the moment I shared my nightmare about those creepy girls in white dresses. Thank you to Charles Beyer for inspiring me with your brilliant Victorian ghost paintings. And to Gary Graham for not only reading parts of an early manuscript, but for the "million-dollar idea" and the subsequent Nightmarys trading-card illustration.

Thank you also to Nico Medina for being a wonderfully perceptive copy editor and an all-around awesome friend. Thank you to Kathy Gersing and Nick Eliopulos for graciously reading the very long first draft and for not wanting to smack me with it. Thanks to Nic DeStefano for the glamorous photo shoot in the Brooklyn Botanic Garden.

Thank you to Katie Cicatelli, Ellice M. Lee, and everyone else at Random House Children's Books, especially my editor, R. Schuyler Hooke, who adopted this baby and helped me make her even more disturbed than she already was. It must be stated that Barry Goldblatt is a dream agent; I'm so grateful he's in my corner. Thank you to David Levithan for all you do.

Thank you to my grandparents, Francis and Wanda Poblocki and Doris and Ray Piehler, for your stories and support. Dad, Maria, Emily, Johnny, Brendan, Amanda, Mom, and Bruce—I love you guys.

And Ethan, you're just the best.

ABOUT THE AUTHOR

In the first nightmare DAN POBLOCKI can remember, giant ants attacked his town. Dan lives in Brooklyn, New York, where he is stalked only by slightly-larger-than-ordinary cockroaches. He is also the author of *The Stone Child*. Visit him at www.danpoblocki.com.